DEATH
ON THE STRIP

Book 1

The Death Card Series

By

J.S. Peck

BEJEWELED PUBLISHING
LAS VEGAS, NEVADA

Bejeweled Publishing
6480 Annie Oakley Drive, Suite 513
Las Vegas, Nevada 89120

ISBN: 978-0-9824607-0-2
First Edition: July 2018

COVER ART DESIGN: Kelly A. Martin
INTERNAL DESIGN: Jake Naylor

DEDICATION

I dedicate the entire Death Card series to my talented sister, Judith Keim, who has taken time away from her successful authoring to help and support me.

"You have been the wind beneath my wings by believing in me and my talent for writing mysteries. When I've been in doubt, all I've had to do was pick up the phone, and you'd patiently share pieces of advice and encouragement. I honor and love you as my twin sister—I'm forever grateful."

Table of Contents

CHAPTER 1

I clicked off the call and sat for a moment in my kitchen as waves of nausea rolled over me. I felt sick. The young woman at the other end sounded desperate to have a reading with me. But the idea of going back to reading tarot cards for clients brought too many painful memories. I wasn't sure I could do it. Guilt for what I hadn't done had stopped any readings because even now, I blamed myself for my fiancé's death. I'd seen the Death card for him and had brushed aside the notion that it meant his death. That decision was still costing me dearly. It would always do so.

Maybe, I thought, the call was a sign to move forward, to get on with my life. I had to remember the Death card was only a warning, announcing the possible demise of someone I knew, had just met, or was soon to meet. The

1

Death card's meaning didn't always signify death—it could be an ending or a new beginning.

I entered my office, got the tarot cards out of my desk drawer, and took them into the kitchen, where I'd meet with the client. I placed them on the table and sat down to wait for her. My heart began to pound as fear washed over me. I thought, What if the Death card shows up? What will I say?

I tried to keep my mind on pleasant things because the tarot cards stirred unwanted memories of Jeff's death and the trouble I'd created when I'd accused the Chief of Police of his death.

It was still painful for me to think back to that time. It seemed like it was just yesterday I was planning my wedding to a man I adored. Jeff was a straight arrow through and through, which became a liability for him. As can happen to people in power, there can be opportunities to take advantage of situations that exceed what is "right" or legal. Jeff had come close to crossing the line. In the end, he opted out.

There had been a drug bust within the police department, and someone had to take the fall. Everyone there was aware that Jeff knew who the players were, and his honesty could take them all down.

In hindsight, it was no surprise that he was found dead in a car accident due to his "falling asleep at the wheel." That was the statement the cops made to the press. I knew that would've never happened. Jeff had more energy than any two people and was cautious in all ways --- especially behind the wheel of a car. Their story didn't ring true by a long shot, and I wanted to prove they were wrong.

I heard a car door slam shut at the same time my pup, Sweet Pea, began to bark. Melissa had arrived. I drew a deep breath and whispered a prayer before letting her in. Sweet Pea danced at Melissa's feet as she came through the door, and she bent down to pat my dog. When Melissa looked up and saw me, she looked surprised, probably expecting someone older.

As she stood in the hallway of my townhouse, she looked around. "Nice," she said before following me into the kitchen. "Your house is so pretty. I'm going to decorate my house like this," she added before sitting down.

"Thank you," I said, picking up the tarot cards from the table. "Shall we get started?"

I didn't know who was more nervous, Melissa or me. The tension built as the beautiful girl sitting across the table waited anxiously for me to turn over one card and another until we came to the last tarot card that would foretell her future. Much to my dismay, as I reached for it, a card came loose from the deck as though someone had jerked it free. We faced the dreaded Death card. My client and I both gasped at the same time. I quickly glanced at her, noting the frown deepening on her brow. I wondered whether she saw what I did—death (perhaps her own?)—all around her. What was I going to say? I needed to be careful with my wording.

"Discernment!" I heard my grandmother whisper from the energy surrounding me. "Discernment, Rosalie!"

I began by saying, "Melissa, the Death card doesn't necessarily mean death. It means something is coming to an end, a change, or new beginnings." I paused. "I saw you in new surroundings, which we haven't discussed yet. Do you want to tell me what that's all about?"

"Well," said Melissa with a sheepish grin, confirming what I'd seen. "I'm starting a new job next week. A real job, a professional job."

"Wow," I said, feeling strangely uneasy. "It sounds as if you're making a big change. What did you do before?" I asked, knowing it wasn't good.

She blushed and said with some defiance, "I was a stripper down on the Las Vegas Strip. That's why you said earlier you saw me dancing, remember?"

Worry began to eat at me. Without hesitating, I asked, "Did you have difficulty getting out of that field? I've heard that sometimes it can be difficult, particularly if drugs are involved at the establishment. "

I watched her face fall. "I'm okay. Anyway, I need to make changes in my life. I'm willing to earn less money to live a decent life—one my mother would be proud of. I want to have a family of my own, too," she added wistfully.

"So, what's your new job?" I asked.

Melissa's face lit up. "I signed up with PUP."

"PUP? What's that?"

Melissa laughed. It stands for Pick Up, the new taxi service, like Uber. You know, the one where I get an alert from PUP, and I pick up the rider in my new car. It's a lot less expensive for them than a regular taxi. The percentage of the money I make is more than I would get if I were a taxicab driver. I even have my own hours! It's a good deal all around."

"Is it safe?" I asked, sounding stodgy and triple my age. "I mean, with strangers in your car?"

My client shrugged her shoulders. Sounding slightly annoyed, she answered, "As safe as any taxi driver, I guess."

"Oh, well. That makes sense, I suppose. And we girls always keep our safety spray handy, don't we?"

She looked at me oddly and said, "Sure, why not?"

4

The rest of her reading and the overview went as well as expected despite the Death card's message looming over us. Melissa talked to me more about planning to change her life since she was only 23. She was looking to create a new home life. As I reviewed with her all the cards' meanings, including the one of a star-crossed love where it would be her choice to be involved—or not—she asked, "Do you see anything bad? I mean, with the Death card?"

"I always tell my clients, with or without the Death card, to become more aware of their surroundings and more sensitive to what their inner body is telling them. Times are different today. Las Vegas is an area with many visitors and transient people. You never know what can happen. The world isn't as safe as it used to be. Just be careful, and follow your inner voice."

She looked at me long and hard. "Okay."

"Keep in touch, and let me know how your new job is going, okay?"

She smiled and said, "Thank you," before grabbing her oversized purse, slinging it over her shoulder, and heading to the door. She turned at the last minute. "I have some things to work out for sure. I might need another reading in a few weeks, okay?"

"Of course. Call me for an appointment, and we'll do this again."

"You did well, Rosie girl," my grandmother said from the mist at my side. "I know you were worried about returning to your readings, but remember, you are there just to guide. It's ultimately up to us to make our own choices, right? Love you, sweetheart. Bye for now."

She faded away. My grandmother amazed me, for she always seemed to know when I needed her, and then, poof, off she'd go, gone until she had something more to say.

It probably seemed strange to most people that my grandmother and I had communicated spiritually since she passed several years ago. She had always been there for me, ever since I was little.

I paused. Looking at the cards, I remembered I'd been just seven years old when I had taken and hidden these same tarot cards from one of an assortment of babysitters assigned to me at the time. I'd been drawn to the cards from the first time I had laid eyes on them. They looked so pretty and magical. However, my mother was furious with me for taking them and told me I was never to touch those cards again. As it turned out, I never did return the cards to that sitter, for she was never asked back. I realize now my mother was upset with me because she feared I'd follow in my grandmother's footsteps with her psychic abilities—something she didn't want to happen.

My parents had been Shakespearean actors traveling the world performing at various less-famous but notable venues until their small plane crashed. I was almost nine at the time. Instead of a nanny to care for me, I had my grandmother on my mother's side, who moved into our house and took over, rearing a shy, introverted little girl—one who knew about things before they happened. It took me a while before I realized she did as well.

She'd say, "Answer the door, Rosie girl!" long before anyone reached our front door.

Or she'd say, "Aunt Mary wants us to go to lunch with her today. You'd better get dressed, Rosie girl!" long before she telephoned with the invitation.

So I began to open up to my grandmother about things that came to me—visions of happenings or simple premonitions. She would simply smile and say, "I know, Rosie girl. You take after me." Then she would hug me tight and tell me how much she loved me, covering my face and neck with kisses. That is when my heart began to open—really open—to all the possibilities of unconditional love and safety within a happy home life.

It wasn't that my parents didn't love me; it was that they were never home to share in my everyday events. And so, in my grandmother's care, I began to blossom. I was a somewhat unusual-looking little girl, an odd mixture of cultures. My grandmother was an Irish gypsy, and I inherited her thick, wild, dark hair. I understood without being told that my mother was somewhat ashamed of my grandmother because of her psychic gifts and dark looks. I guess it was one of the reasons I hadn't spent much time with her before she moved in to take care of me.

On the other hand, my mother was thrilled that I had also inherited my father's green eyes and pinkish-white skin, so I was more the color of an apricot. Like many attractive women my age, I saw myself with a mop of unruly hair and a mind of its own. Some might call me a natural beauty today, but I didn't see myself that way.

As I became older, I grew to 5′ 10″ and lost my pudginess and some of my awkwardness. I began to understand that my psychic abilities were a gift to be used cautiously. Many people fear anything psychic, including my classmates— especially the boys, once they discovered I had those abilities. I learned the hard way that not everyone wants to be warned of things before they happen, especially if the news isn't good.

One time in junior high school, I lost my temper. I walked up to the boy who was taunting me and punched him in the eye, making him the laughingstock of the entire school. I had been a brat to him, calling him names and becoming the bully to him that he was to me. The whole incident caused an uproar, with people taking sides. Truth be told, I was very pleased with myself.

My grandmother was certainly not pleased to be called to the school office to claim her granddaughter, who had a dirty trail of tears running down her face. She was more upset with me that I had stooped to his level and had fought back. I could hear her mumbling, "She's just a child. She doesn't understand the consequences of what she's doing ...."

Later, I found out that my gram visited the boy in high school who had been the worst bully and had made me unhappy enough to skip school. That stopped any bullying—and even any kind of friendship. I never knew what happened, but from then on, no one bothered me again, which, unfortunately, included most of the kids in my class. To say the least, it was a very difficult time for me during those school years and even later. I hate to admit it now, but it must have also been hard on my grandmother. Others ridiculed her in town, yet many of those same critical women sneaked into our house for a tarot card reading with her.

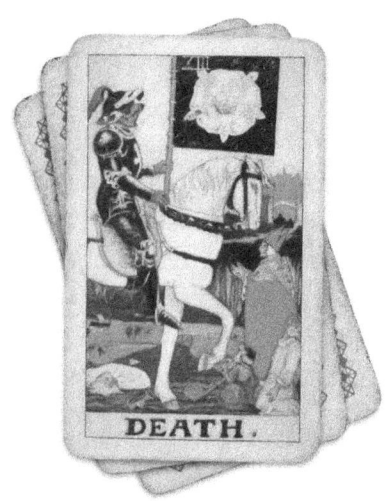

CHAPTER 2

A few weeks later, after my reading with Melissa, I was getting ready to fly to Los Angeles. I was going to meet with Sarah, the editor of *Women Living Well*, a magazine to which I submitted monthly mind/body/spirit articles. I always looked forward to our meetings, as she and I were in sync with our thoughts and beliefs. However, traveling that day was not the fun it used to be, especially with spending more time waiting in terminals than flying. I had the idea I'd call PUP for a ride to the airport to try them out. Hoping to have Melissa as my driver this time, I used the app I had downloaded on my phone and waited for a response. I looked at my watch to make sure I was calling in plenty of time for my request to be met.

"Who's there?" demanded a deep, gruff male voice.

"Is this the number for PUP?" I asked, confused.

"Sorry about that," a sweet female voice cut in. "Where are you heading?"

"To the airport. I want to request Melissa Johnson if she's available. Tell her it's Rosie."

"I'll see. She's swamped lately. Let me check."

As I waited for her response, I thought it odd she was that busy. Didn't they usually let the drivers who have been there the longest get better rides? Or isn't that the way it worked? I had no idea.

"I got hold of her. She says she knows where you live. She'll be by within the next 20 minutes. Is that okay?" asked the same sweet voice.

"Sure. I'll be ready," I responded, glad Melissa would take me for my first ride with PUP.

I talked to my little Silky Terrier dog, Sweet Pea, telling her not to worry because I would be back later that night. With tail down, she left me, heading to her dog bed, unhappy to be staying home. Precisely 20 minutes later, Melissa pulled up in her brand-new blue Honda CV-R. I could hear grumbling coming from the back seat of the car.

"Come on, lady, hurry it up. I've got a plane to catch."

"Why do you think I'm going to the airport?" I fumed under my breath. I gave him a pained expression and shook my head in irritation. "Hold on, Cowboy, I'm coming."

As Melissa took my carry-on luggage, the man jumped out of his seat to help her lift it into the back of the car. I opened the other door to the back seat and hopped in. The man climbed back in and scowled at me, irritating me even more.

"What's your problem, Cowboy?" I asked. I had no patience with rude people.

"I'm a reporter. I have to catch my flight to Reno, and since we had to pick you up, I'll probably miss it."

"Really," I said with disgust. "Don't worry. You're not going to miss your flight, so calm down."

"How do you know?" he asked with annoyance. When Melissa and I locked eyes in the car's rearview mirror,

I noticed she had a black eye. She saw me staring and immediately turned away. All is not well, I thought. Too bad.

I returned to my fellow passenger, giving him the once-over. Nice-looking. No, I thought, more than that. He was really handsome with his deep red, curly hair and bright blue eyes. He acted like he knew it too.

I turned away to look out the window and get a grip on my thoughts. Strange, I hadn't been interested in any man since my former fiancé, Jeff, died three years ago. And now, this very irritating man had stirred my thoughts. Enough! I admonished myself. You don't have time for this. Besides, a man in your life is the last thing you need! They are nothing but trouble.

The reporter readied himself and his backpack to immediately jump out of the car. As we pulled curbside of Terminal A, he bounded out. His business card fell to the vehicle's floor as he did so. I picked it up. His name was Brian Boyce. He handed a wad of cash to Melissa and raced away through the swinging doors. I opened my door and headed to the back of the car to collect my bag. Melissa met me there and pulled out the bag, tucking her head into the turned-up collar of her jacket to hide her face.

"Melissa, if you're in trouble or need help, please let me help you."

"I'm okay," she muttered. "Just don't let my boss know there were two of you in the car for the airport ride, okay? He doesn't know I picked up a side job, and I don't want to get in trouble."

11

I nodded my head. "Just be careful. Don't put up with anything or anyone who doesn't treat you right, do you hear?" I warned. "Remember my offer," I added. "Call me if you need me."

Melissa nodded and moved to the front of the car— but not before I saw a tear running down her cheek. She straightened her shoulders and climbed into the driver's seat. She pulled away as I stood there watching her go. With a deep sigh, I entered the terminal to go through security and head to my gate.

My thoughts traveled to Melissa and her obvious plight. I'd had only one other client in her line of business. It hadn't ended well. The Death card had come up in her reading too, and later, she was found dead of an overdose. I vowed at that time not to get involved again with a stripper. And now, here I was, stretching out a hand to Melissa. Sometimes it seemed that I never learned.

The trips to Los Angeles to meet Sarah at the magazine's office were usually fun. That day was different. I was still thinking about Melissa and her situation when I reached Los Angeles. I ran into a couple arguing outside the *Women Living Well* offices. They were young and seemed high on something.

I heard the girl say, "Ow! Why did you slap me?"

"Because you pissed me off," he answered. "I told you before not to keep asking me for a hit. I've given you enough."

"Just one more," she pleaded, stepping back so he couldn't reach her.

The guy looked at me and hollered, "What are you looking at, bitch? Why don't you mind your own business? C'mon, let's get out of here," he said, pulling the girl along with him.

What the heck? What's going on? What is the world coming to?" I wondered as I walked into the building. I thought about how happy I was, holed up in my little house, writing my column and doing my readings, escaping life. Those days were gone. I felt incomplete and yearned for more. I lived a somewhat safe, boring life—a pretty selfish one, escaping life. Thank God I was finally beginning to get interested in living a much fuller life again. Isn't it about time? I berated myself.

As soon as she saw me, Sarah bounced out of her office. She threw her arms around me. "I'm so glad to see you, Rosie. I've got some exciting news! We're going to take our magazine up a notch and do more reality stories. I want you to be the first one on board. C'mon in so I can explain."

I sat wide-eyed with excitement as she explained. "I have the approval of the entire magazine staff to expand what we do to address more fully what you and I both know is how things are playing out today. There's so much physical and verbal violence from men toward women and vice versa. Even words of songs strongly devalue women or call us bitches. No one seems to say anything nice anymore. Have we all lost our sense of courtesy? We want to step up our magazine to recognize and talk about the world as it is. Are you with me?"

"Well, it's certainly about time to have more pushback. What exactly is it you want me to do?"

"I was thinking that since you live in Las Vegas, you could report on what's *really* going on there. I'm sure that'll provide you with plenty of material. Since we are a magazine about women, we're trying to bring to the forefront that it is we women who have the power to demand changes in how we are treated and represented, whether it's sexually, financially, or any other way. You could feature those who have made a difference. That extends to all the other issues as well. We're asking you to become more aware of "what's hip" in Las Vegas. We want both the glamorous and even the seamier side. Then report to us what you've learned—in the form of a monthly column."

Sarah stopped just long enough to catch her breath. "Oh, and also address how women can be more effective in changing society for the better. Of course, that also means featuring some of the shakers and movers in Vegas doing just that—both female and male. You could use a different name to separate yourself from your current column. But perhaps you can give it a twist with your mind/body/spirit. Would this work for you? Are you interested?" she asked with excitement. "Oh, please say yes."

A headache began to form as I remembered the incident with the couple outside the magazine's offices. "Well, let me think about it."

"We'd pay you your regular rate; you may receive more if it takes off. Of course, as usual, you'd still have your spiritual column with your name and byline. Please send us some potential articles in the next month or so. We want to review them before we change the slant of the magazine with what you and some others will be contributing."

Although I'd worked with Sarah for quite a while now, she had no idea I was intuitive and read tarot cards. Maybe that would be an advantage for me. Could I do a good enough job for them? Yes, this certainly would be a challenge. I'd become even more secluded since Jeff's death. I tended to hide behind my writing, and I'd not been willing to step out and steep myself in the negative energies of living in today's world.

My grandmother whispered, "This will bring some excitement into your life, and you will be helping others simply in a different way."

I waved away the interference of my grandmother's voice and looked up to see Sarah staring at me questioningly. "Is that your answer? No?"

"Oh, no," I countered. "Just brushing some hair away." We both knew it was time for me to step out of my self-made shell and do more. "If you believe I can do what you want, you can count on me. I'm willing to give it at least a try."

"Wonderful!" cried Sarah. "I knew you'd want to be a part of this. We'll send you the outline of what we are looking for and the contract covering all aspects of this new assignment. Let's grab some lunch to get caught up on other things, okay?"

I arrived home with an air of excitement. I was glad I'd be doing something different. There was no question I'd have much to learn. Becoming a Las Vegas reporter was exciting, just in a scary way. I hoped I made the right choice to charge ahead. Time will tell.

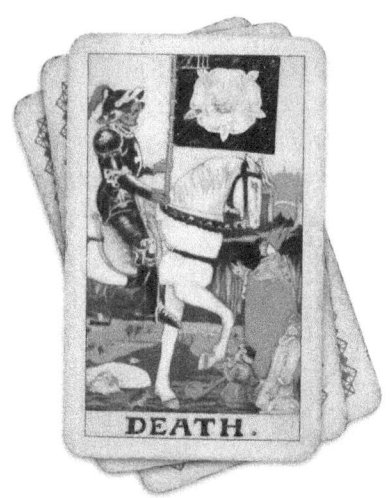

CHAPTER 3

For the second morning in a row, I woke up exhausted from a night of tossing and turning. I was excited about the prospect of my new writing assignment for the magazine, and I grabbed my robe and headed downstairs. I let Sweet Pea out back to do her thing, and then I headed to the front door to retrieve the newspaper that usually awaited me. As I bent down to pick it up, I saw a fat, tan envelope stuffed halfway under the doormat. I grabbed it and the newspaper and entered the house, tossing the newspaper onto the kitchen counter.

I clasped the bulging envelope with my first name written across it while I searched for a knife to slit it open. I was anxious to see what was inside. As I emptied it, dollar bills flew everywhere. Then a white envelope with "Mom" written on it and a scrap of white notepaper dropped to the floor. I picked up the small sheet of paper and saw a handwritten note.

"Rosie, you were right. It's not so easy getting out of my kind of business. I'm going to need your help after all. I'll call you later today to explain so we can make arrangements. Meanwhile, if something happens to me, please be sure my mother gets this money and her letter. Thanks—Melissa." Her mother's address was at the bottom.

I gathered the bills and counted them—$23,345. Wow! That's quite a pile for a PUP driver, I thought. As I studied the money, I saw several men arguing with Melissa, so the cash seemed not likely from PUP. Oh, damn! Now what?

I began to read the letter to her mother and returned it to its envelope when I saw, "I'm sorry, Mom, for all the trouble I caused you ...." That was personal and not anything related to me or something I had a right to read.

I made coffee and turned on the TV to watch the morning news. It was going to be a hot day, which was no surprise, as it was May weather. The president would give a speech that night on the economy—what a roller coaster ride! The female commentator's voice broke in as she announced another murder had occurred the night before in Las Vegas. She said the victim had been beaten and left beside the road next to her car with the engine still running.

As I looked at the car, I recognized the blue Honda CR-V. I knew then who the victim was—Melissa. My stomach roiled as the coffee turned to acid inside my belly. I sat on the couch, catching my breath and calming myself. My heart sank. Poor Melissa.

I knew my first story about what was happening in Las Vegas was going to be about her death, maybe about any possible connection with her being a stripper here in

Las Vegas. I felt her death must have something to do with that. I desperately wanted to discover what had happened to her and why, yet I wasn't exactly sure where to begin. Clearly, I should start at the scene of the crime. I hurried to shower and get dressed before heading to the crime scene.

When I arrived in the old downtown, the police had cordoned off the area with yellow tape. The forensic team was doing its thing. I stepped into the middle of the crowd that had gathered outside the barricades to try to pick up some gossip or news. In a few of my favorite "whodunit" novels, I had read that the perpetrator would often come to the crime scene to view his (or her?) work. I searched each face in the crowd, looking for clues. I stopped dead when I saw the rude PUP passenger staring back at me in surprise.

He pushed a few people away from him and came toward me. "What are you doing here? A little sightseeing?"

"I might ask the same question of you, Cowboy," I said, annoyance building in me.

"Touché," he responded, seeming oddly pleased at my reaction.

"Well, then?" I pushed. "What have you found out? Have they caught the person responsible for Melissa's death?"

"So you knew her. Hmmm. And what about you? What do you know?"

"Nothing," I answered grumpily, not wanting him to report my name connecting me to the murder.

He looked at me long and hard. "Look, I know I was a bit of a dick on the ride to the airport. I apologize. Let's start again. My name is Brian Boyce. Pleased to meet you."

As he held out his hand, I took it and demurely said, "My name is Rosalie Bennett," omitting the pleased part.

19

He grudgingly accepted my rudeness. "I already know who you are. I looked you up on Google." Seeing my surprised expression, he added, "I saw your name tag on your carry-on case when I put it into the trunk of Melissa's car." He began to turn away. I pulled at his sleeve, asking, "So, what have you learned about this crime? I want to know."

"Not much to tell yet. Anything you can tell me?" she was a stripper at the Purple Passion Club before she signed on with PUP.

"Nothing. We weren't friends, more like acquaintances," I answered, not about to say more.

He stared at me for a moment, squinting at me. "Are you sure you're not hiding anything?"

"Of course not!" I exclaimed indignantly. I wasn't about to mention the money and the package Melissa had left with me.

"Just asking," he said, holding his palms in front of him defensively.

I could feel my face turn red. This man could infuriate me without even trying. "Don't you have some reporting to do, Cowboy?"

"I kinda like you calling me Cowboy, you know. I can conjure up a lot of pleasant thoughts with that one, if you know what I mean," he teased, wiggling his eyebrows up and down.

I had enough and turned away from him. "Happy riding!" I called out. I heard him chuckle as I walked away. What was it about that man that got me so rattled? Brian was undoubtedly handsome, for several women had turned to admire him when he walked toward me.

I figured he was probably close to my age—32—maybe even a bit older and probably married, although I hadn't

20

noticed a ring. I wasn't even curious about finding out. I wasn't interested in getting involved with any man right now, not even someone as good-looking as Brian. Jeff's death left me devastated. I was still healing from all the anger his demise had created. I'd learned that a relationship easily distracts me from doing my own thing, with its demands pulling at my time and energy. Besides, I had too much I wanted to do to clear Jeff's name, and now there was Melissa's murderer to be brought to justice.

When I got home, I began to worry about the money Melissa had left with me. I knew I should probably report it to the police, but something kept holding me back. Besides, I wasn't ready to release it without knowing where it had come from and whether it was legitimate. I didn't trust the police because of all that happened in the past, and they probably would take it from me before I could find out what I wanted to know. I wasn't willing to let that happen.

I had a special hiding place I'd fashioned beneath the floor in my closet that I was certain no one would find. I even had difficulty relocating it anytime I needed to get into it. I put Melissa's money into the hidden space and replaced the things surrounding it. Then I went to do some research on my computer for my magazine articles. I even ordered the book *The Las Vegas Madame* by Jami Rodman. That should be an eye-opener since I knew little about the escort business and how it all worked.

Later, everything that happened during the day was exhausting, so I decided to quit while I was ahead.

I had an early supper and went to bed, hoping I wouldn't have any dreams to keep me awake. I knew more upset was to come.

CHAPTER 4

T he following day, I wanted to get a head start on my new assignment for the magazine. Sitting at my desk, I looked up and read a favorite quote I had found shortly after Jeff's death taped to my computer.

"Learn to love with all your heart and accept the unlovable side of others, for anyone can love a rose, but it takes a great heart to include the thorns."

As I stared at that quote, I knew these words would take on greater meaning when I went into the streets of Las Vegas as a self-declared sleuth, writing for the magazine— and keeping my promise to clear Jeff's name. I kept it there to ground me and to make me appreciate the individual journey of each person who came to me.

I love Las Vegas, for it's an exciting city. Years ago, it was a valued stopover, allowing those in covered wagons and other travelers to refill their water supply from the many open springs. As it has grown and sits today, Las Vegas has its charm as a diverse city of extremes between its spiritual natural resources and man-created debauchery.

Nevada is the only jurisdiction in the United States where prostitution is legal. Las Vegas gets a bad rap, for it's so much more than all that.

Next, I began researching the internet to see what I could find on strippers or prostitution. I paused. I had to be careful that what I wrote in an article for the magazine was accurate. All this was too much for me. I didn't have enough knowledge to write about this and wasn't sure this was what Sarah meant for my column.

I looked at my watch and couldn't believe how much time had passed. Now I needed to concentrate more on what had happened to Melissa and what the world of being a stripper was like. As a stripper, wasn't Melissa most likely under the power of a man who was her boss? Was her death simply because she was an exotic dancer, as the press was now indicating? I wondered.

The phone interrupted my thoughts. I answered with a cautious "Hello?"

"Is this Rosalie Bennett?" a voice whispered.

"Yes, it is. How can I help you?"

"I'm a friend of Melissa. I need to talk to you in person. Is there somewhere we can meet?" she asked worriedly.

"Can you come to my house?"

"No, I don't think it's safe for you if I come there."

Alarm made me ask, "Are you in danger? Are you all right?"

"Yeah, I'm okay, or I will be if you can help me."

"Can't you talk to me now?"

"I'm not in a place where it's safe to talk. Let's meet somewhere where no one will know we are together. Some place like the Bellagio?"

"Why me?" I asked with hesitation. "Why don't you go to the police?"

"I can't do that. Melissa said you were cool and could be trusted."

"Okay," I said with a deep sigh. "I guess I can meet you. What time?"

"Now is a good time. Can you meet me now?"

"All right. How will I recognize you?"

"I think you'll recognize me right away. I'll be in a ponytail with a red bow and a tiny butterfly tattoo on my neck. My name is Sally Smith, by the way."

"Do you want to know what I look like?"

"No, I looked you up on the internet. I'll recognize you."

We made final arrangements for where to meet, and I hurried around, wondering whether I was heading into danger. I pulled my hair back, gathered it at my neck, and topped it with a baseball cap. Then I put on a lightweight jacket with a hood to cover me up as much as possible. Would I need a weapon of some sort? I grabbed my large purse, security spray, and iPhone, which could record our conversation if required.

I gave Sweet Pea one of her special treats and assured her that dogs weren't allowed or I would be happy to have her join me. She just stared at me sadly. She never truly believes she is a dog and wonders why I tell her that. She thinks she's one of the girls in my group of friends.

"Oh well," I sighed. "I'll be back soon," I called out as I headed out the door.

I hadn't been to the Bellagio Hotel and Casino in a while but found it as beautiful as ever. The beautiful glass sculpture of flowers called Fiori di Como, created by glass sculptor Dale Chihuly hangs from the large, 18-foot-high ceiling of their reception area. This exquisite piece of art, with its rich bursts of color and flowers of various sizes, lifted my heart each time I entered the hotel and feasted my eyes on it.

The foyer held several huge pots of gorgeous flower arrangements, the largest and the most beautiful I had ever seen. Beyond were the seasonal gardens. They were another treat, a showstopper with creative sets and themes. They were decorated in concert with the current season and filled with magnificent live flowers in scenes beyond the imagination. Although it took up to a year to develop a seasonal creation, it took only a few nights to transform the space into an outstanding result that drew crowds of tourists and us locals. We looked forward to gazing at every gift of inspiration, capturing them with cameras. I was no exception. Seeing this never-ending splendor was always worth the trip to the strip.

Walking through the casino that day, I saw live birds in a greenhouse in the center of this new scenario. Each bird was chirping its tune, flying around, and landing on various plants, bird feeders, and the like.

I quickly walked beyond these gardens and continued down the hall. I passed the chocolate fountain and the treats that abounded inside the glass cases to tempt anyone who passed by. I loved chocolate and usually would stop to collect a piece or two of my favorite, almond brittle. Not that day. I was anxious to meet with Sally. I wanted to hear what she had to say.

I spotted the ladies' room just beyond the theater and headed toward it, looking around to see whether we'd be alone. It seemed so, for it was quiet, with nobody else in sight. Inside the bathroom, I spotted a single pair of feet in the stall at the far end. I called out, "Hello?"

When she came out, she looked scared. "I think I was followed."

Amazing! I thought as I took her in. I would have had to be blind not to have noticed her photo, much less not recognize her. For better or for worse, she was easy to identify, with her blond hair, blue eyes, and oversized breasts. Her body was displayed on one of the traveling billboard trucks that advertised sex and constantly drove throughout the city.

I felt a warning that something wasn't right. "Sally?" I whispered, "Is it all right to talk here? Are we alone?"

Her face fell, and she repeated, "I think I may have been followed."

As I stood there, she reached out and grabbed my arm. She pulled me into the far corner of the restroom. Her voice quivering, she said, "Listen, I need to ask you something. The other night Melissa told me she was taking what she needed to leave the business and Vegas for good. Did she say anything to you about going? Did she tell you anything about taking something that didn't belong to her?"

As I waited to respond, I saw a vision of Sally arguing with a man. I knew without question Sally was in trouble.

Sally whispered, "Melissa was my friend. You can trust me."

"Don't tell her anything, Rosie," my grandmother whispered, interfering.

"Did Melissa tell you why she was leaving?" I asked Sally.

"I think she had something going on, but I don't know what. I know she had a problem with the lounge managers at the end. They said she wasn't doing enough to keep the clients happy. She was sad and upset, though. She told me her heart wasn't in it any longer."

"Melissa had a black eye. What was that all about?"

"That happens sometimes," she said, waving that away.

"Did she have a boyfriend?" I asked, urging her on.

"Look, I'm sorry. I don't have all the answers. I came here to ask if you knew anything about Melissa taking something that wasn't hers, that's all! I need to find what's missing; that's it! Please answer the question, yes or no?"

Something wasn't making sense. The amount of money in Melissa's envelope wasn't large enough for Sally's boss to worry about in the overall scheme of things. The private letter to her mom and even the note to me was personal and none of anyone's business as far as I was concerned. So I answered, "Unfortunately, no. She never mentioned to me taking anything that wasn't hers," twisting the truth by not mentioning the money. "What did she take anyhow?"

"Nothing for you to worry about," she added. "I didn't think you knew anything or were involved in any way."

"What's going to happen now?" I asked.

"I dunno. I can't believe this all has happened, you know?" she responded genuinely sadly.

"Yes, I know what you mean. It's unbelievable to think that Melissa was beaten to death. And for what? I can't understand it. Why would someone do that?"

Sally was quiet, shaking her head, saying nothing.

"Well, then, Sally, since there's nothing more to say, I guess I'll be on my way. You have my telephone number. Will you let me know if there will be a service or anything for Melissa?"

Sally looked at me with sad eyes. "I'll try calling you later," she whispered in a subdued voice.

"Be careful," I whispered back so quietly it would be impossible for anyone else to hear. "I'll leave first; then you follow in a couple of minutes, okay?"

She agreed. I covered my face as much as possible before leaving the restroom. I was curious to see if anyone had followed Sally. I knew a place beside the theater where I could hide to see whether anyone would approach Sally when she left the ladies' room. All I had to do was slip into that spot without anyone taking notice. I looked around and saw no one, so I tucked myself in and waited.

Five long minutes passed before I saw Sally emerge from the bathroom. As soon as she did, a dark-haired man approached her from the other end of the hall. He grabbed her and tightly held onto her left arm, pushing her forward. They were arguing. I couldn't see his face, but his hairstyle was a bit unusual, reminiscent of the 1930s. Perhaps I'd be able to recognize him again.

Sally looked unhappy and complained to the man, "Why are you holding onto me like this? I told you I don't know anything!"

I couldn't hear what the man whispered to her, but Sally relaxed and stopped struggling because several women were walking toward them. Behind them, there were even more women chatting and laughing with each other as they approached. When I became stalled amid them, I lost track of Sally and her escort. One of the conference sessions must have been let out, and the women were refreshing themselves in the ladies' room.

Damn! It was time to head home and see whether the tarot cards could shed some light on my increasing concern for Sally. What would they reveal?

CHAPTER 5

I arrived home wrapped in concern about what I was sensing. I didn't think the ramifications of Melissa's death would go away anytime soon. I could feel there was more to come. Things weren't right and hadn't been since the first moment I sat with Melissa and the tarot cards. Things weren't adding up. Where did the money come from? What did Sally mean when she said she didn't know about anything else? What was holding me back from reporting this to the police? I could be in serious trouble for keeping it quiet. Was I willing to take that risk? How did Sally fit into all of this? Why did I feel Sally was being used as a pawn by the person involved in Melissa's death? What was the link between all of them?

No Sweet Pea greeted me when I opened the back door from the garage into the house. *She must still be upset, waiting in her chair for me to greet her.* As I rounded into the living room, there she was, resting on the overstuffed leather chair with one eye open. Sweet Pea stared at me, waiting for my welcome. I went to her, calling out, "Hi there, baby girl, I'm home," giving her hugs and kisses—doing the opposite of what most dog training books advised you to do when greeting your dog. Her tail wagged, and she seemed to forgive me for leaving her behind.

I left her to collect my tarot cards. As I was shuffling the cards, my mind wandered. How was I going to find out more about Melissa's life? Did she have a roommate? Was there anyone I could trust, perhaps another of Melissa's friends?

"Turn on the TV news," my grandmother whispered.

I hurriedly slammed my tarot cards on the table, raced to the television, and turned it on. When I did, a single tarot card fell onto the floor; perhaps a warning? I ignored it. I'll have to look at it later, I thought, as I turned up the volume on the TV. There was an attractive blond girl, looking a little worn and tired. She was answering questions from the reporters who surrounded her. Right in the midst of it was Brian Boyce. "Of course, he would be the center of attention," I muttered, unreasonably annoyed.

"So, Mary," he asked, "You said you didn't see Melissa at all during the day and evening before she died?"

"No. I slept in that morning because it had been a late night." She stood there before Brian, her expression bright, obviously pleased with the attention he was giving her.

"Did you and Melissa get along as roommates? Were you close?"

This time, Mary began fluttering her eyes at Brian, acting coy before finally speaking. "I guess you can say we were close. We shared the same life."

"Mary, I know you must be upset with Melissa's death. Do you know of anyone who would want her dead?" Brian asked.

The camera came close to Mary's face. She knows something, I thought, and I am going to find out what! Although she enjoyed the attention, her eyes barely flickered, and her pupils enlarged as Brian asked his question.

When Mary began to shake her head no to the question, Brian stepped fully into the camera's view. "Folks, there will be more news to come as the details of this ghastly murder unfolds. Over and out." Brian Boyce, Channel 5.

I stepped back from the television and watched the following news story. It showed an angry man. He had returned to his ex-girlfriend's house in a jealous rage and killed both her and her mother, who had been visiting her. All that despite a restraining order she had against him. I felt sick. I usually don't watch the news because it's so violent. That just reinforced why I didn't. Restraining orders—they never seemed to work, I fumed. Down the road, who knew? Maybe that would be another excellent topic for my new column in *Women Living Well*.

I returned to the table and picked up the tarot card that had dropped onto the floor. The Death card, of course. Why wouldn't it be, with all the crazy things happening around me? "Enough. Back to research," I muttered.

I sat in front of my computer, wondering where to start. Is anything confidential anymore? I doubted it. You've got to love computers today, for they are the blabbermouths of our society and those worldwide.

I typed in the Purple Passion Lounge and was surprised there wasn't much there. The site required a password to get beyond the home page. That page showed Sally in a provocative stance—all bum and tits. The background showed the lounge area, glowing with garish purple lights so gaudy they made me wonder whether clowns ready to perform were waiting in the background.

Next, I Googled the name Sally Smith in Nevada. I came up with hundreds. I narrowed it down to Las Vegas, Nevada, and came up with more than 20, including some repeats and listings of those who had died. I went through the five who seemed plausible. Sure enough, I found Sally's pictures, tying her to the Purple Passion Lounge and the traveling advertising truck. She was in her famous pose in all of them, of course. She wasn't the only girl to work for the lounge, yet she seemed to be the only one representing it. Why is that? I thought. And who was the owner of the nightclub?

I felt Sweet Pea at my knee, letting me know it was time to quit working. I looked at the clock and saw it was time to stop—time for her dinner and a glass of wine for me.

I intended to call Melissa's mother in the morning to express my condolences. I wasn't sure yet whether I would mention the money, but perhaps I'd be able to learn more about Melissa's life in Las Vegas from her mother. Maybe she could help me understand why Melissa had been murdered.

I was exhausted. Right after dinner, I fell asleep watching one of the addictive series on Netflix. I awoke with a start. Sweet Pea was barking at loud knocking on the front door. I tried to get my bearings as

I headed downstairs to quiet the racket and see who was pounding on the door.

I peeked through the peephole and was amazed to see Brian Boyce. What was it with this man? Why was he here?

"What is it?" I called through the door.

I heard him chuckle. "Are you going to keep talking to me through the closed door, or are you going to let me in?"

"What for? What do you want?" I asked in a grumpy voice.

"Rosie, I'm not going to bite. I just want to talk to you. Please open the door. It's important. You can keep it open while we stand here and talk."

I opened the door just a crack. Sweet Pea nosed her way out, all excited to have someone else with us. She quickly becomes bored with just me. As usual, Sweet Pea thought Brian was there to see her. She responded to that idea by dancing and prancing around him. He was delighted and reciprocated by oohing and aahing over her, exclaiming about what an adorable, beautiful little dog she was. As all the cooler air inside the house went out through the open door, I thought it was time to stop this lovefest. "Okay, Cowboy, come on in."

We sat at the glass kitchen table, where he leaned forward, looking me in the eye. "I know that you're concerned about what happened to Melissa. You may not realize anyone digging around will discover she'd visited you here a few weeks earlier. They'll want to know why. So do I."

I stared at Brian, not knowing what to say.

"Are you hiding something, Rosie girl?" he asked, using my grandmother's exact pet phrase.

I could see concern growing in Brian's eyes as I hesitated rather than answer his question. "Rosie, if you are hiding something, you could be in trouble. That doesn't make me very happy."

"How does that affect you?" I retorted, amazed at the idea.

"Look, I don't like seeing any woman get hurt, and let's leave it at that. I'm not sure you realize how important this would be for me if I could break the case. Especially before the police do."

I sensed how badly he wanted to be the hero who caught the criminal, but I wasn't ready to spill the beans about Melissa's money. I waited, knowing there was more to come.

"Let's make a deal then. Are you interested in hearing what I have to say?"

"Sure, why not?" I answered without much enthusiasm. "I know you cared about your friend Melissa and want justice served. That women thing, right?"

I nodded in response, wondering where he was going with that.

"In my research on you, I know you and your grandmother helped the police with your psychic abilities in the past. My sources say you even helped bring down the Grim Sleeper serial killer of Los Angeles, right?"

Again, I nodded my head reluctantly.

"Then, why not work together? As a woman, you'll be able to find out some things that I can't, and vice versa. Two heads are better than one anyway, right?"

"I don't know what you're really asking me to do or how I can help you."

"I think we can make a great team! We'll be working off the grid, which I don't think will be that unusual for you, and …."

Trying to envision how this could open the door for me and my new assignment for the magazine, I interrupted. "Let me think about it for a day or two."

"Fair enough," he responded. "Just don't take too long because time is flying by, you know?"

He eased Sweet Pea off his lap and rose from the chair he had sidled onto. Reaching into his pocket, he pulled out his business card. "My cell phone number is on here. If anything comes up, please call me. Just be careful. The kind of thing done to Melissa is by someone who has no scruples. They aren't afraid of a pretty thing like you. Believe me; I know."

As he watched me roll my eyes at his comment, he continued. "I know you're poking around, so I will repeat it—watch out! You don't know what viper's nest you can step into. And for heaven's sake, call me if you need me."

Brian stepped closer. Before I could protest, he reached for the back of my head and pulled me toward him. He ended up simply kissing me on the forehead in a brotherly way. Brian patted Sweet Pea and left through the front door without looking back.

Did it make sense for me to team up with Brian? We never addressed the reason Melissa had come to my house. I wasn't sure how I felt about anything that had occurred, so with thoughts reeling, I scooped up Sweet Pea to turn in for the night.

CHAPTER 6

I tossed and turned all night long, so much so that Sweet Pea heaved a sigh of frustration and left my side to stretch out at the foot of the bed. I understood. All my tossing and turning had annoyed me as well.

I awoke feeling panicky, almost afraid to close my eyes again. Weird dreams plagued me all night, causing me to stifle screams of protest. Many of my dreams were of me trying to run, with feet heavy as cement, from an unidentifiable source.

Jeff's face mingled with Brian's, becoming one in many of these dreams. I had once read that dreams were to balance your mind and thoughts. I hoped that wasn't true, for I couldn't imagine how my nightmares were possibly helping me balance anything in my life! Instead, they were upsetting me. I rolled over and got out of bed. I decided to start my day despite having no great urge to do so.

As I sat with my morning coffee, I began to meditate. What was I thinking? The idea of partnering with the most irritating guy I have ever met astounded me. Yet, something was urging me to consider it. Plus, it would make interesting content for my new magazine column.

As much as he thought I was hiding something from him, I felt as strongly that he was hiding something from me. I saw a broken heart when I closed my eyes and concentrated on his image. I wondered what that was all about. What's going on? Maybe it was time to find out.

I showered, dressed, and decided to see whether Brian was free to meet me for a glass of wine at the local roadhouse not too far from where I lived.

He picked up on the first ring. "What's happening?" he asked, using his famous greeting.

"Cowboy, it's Rosalie." I could hear what sounded like a chair being scraped back, as if he were straightening up, coming to attention.

"Hi, Rosie. Have you made up your mind about the … you know what?"

"Not yet. But let's discuss your idea further. Can you meet me for a wine at Sam's Roadhouse tonight? Say around 5:30?"

"For you, always, Rosie girl."

"Good. See you later then." I hung up before he could ask me anything more.

"Gram, I know you're around," I called out. "I can feel you smiling. Don't make more out of this than it is. Hear me?"

I felt a puff of air and knew she had taken off again. I thought it might be a good idea to get out my tarot cards and pick my card for the day to see what it would convey.

I shuffled the cards and spread them out on the kitchen table. I chose a single card from the pile, the Two of Cups.

That was a very interesting card, I thought. Its love and relationship aspect means you should let your soul spread its wings, talk things over, and reconcile, among other things. A partnership. That's exactly what I hoped to do with Brian—talk things over and perhaps spread my wings.

As I went to gather the cards to put them back into their special pouch, a card fell onto the floor. I knew what it was before I even picked it up. Sure enough—the Death card. The first person who came to mind was Sally. This time goosebumps spread across my entire body—a sign of truth and prediction. I felt a little sick.

Please, God, no more deaths like Melissa's, I prayed. The only way I knew to reach Sally was to dial the number left on my phone from the day before when she had called me. I dialed it, not knowing what I could say wouldn't sound dumb. But I didn't need to worry. Instead of reaching Sally's private number, I got a recording saying my message could not be received. Had she called from a public phone booth?

I busied myself working on my next body/mind/ spirit article for the magazine. This time I would explain in further depth how the Law of Attraction works and how to use it for your highest good. Of course, it works the same for negative energy. It amazes me how powerful we are when we send loving energy out and have that love energy returned to us in many ways from many sources.

The day slipped by, with Sweet Pea coming to get me at her usual time of 4:30 p. m. to let me know enough was enough. It was now time to play with her before dinner. The thing about Sweet Pea is that I don't need to wear a watch, for she has her inner timing device that's pretty accurate. I never even set my morning alarm anymore.

I dressed more carefully than usual and applied a touch of mascara and eye shadow. My cheeks were pink enough. I didn't need lipstick, for my lips were naturally rosy. Besides, is anything more annoying than having your lipstick coat on the outside of your wine glass? Some thought it sexy. I did not.

When I got to Sam's Roadhouse, I was pleased to see Brian was already there. He grinned and gave me a thumbs-up, probably because I was early. He waved me over to his table, tucked into the corner of the bar area.

I slid into the seat across from him, saying, "Hello there!"

"Hi! What's your poison? Red or white?"

"I would love a glass of their specialty, Syrah from Australia, please."

"Nice choice!" Brian said as he called the waitress over. "How about some of their nice shrimp cocktail to nibble on?"

I nodded in agreement and waited for him to finish with our order. Then, he turned to me. "So what are you thinking, Rosie?"

During the day, I thought hard and long about our possible partnership. I had no clear idea of his motive beyond the obvious. Something was driving him, and I wanted to know what it was. The waitress came with our wine and shrimp. After she left, I said, "Cowboy, you seem to be hiding something from me."

"Just trust me, okay?" he asked as he winked.

"It's not a simple matter of trust to me. It's a matter of knowing enough about each other to trust each other."

"Okay," he said with a twinkle in his eyes. "You start, and I'll see whether you can tell me something I don't already know."

"Already know? What do you mean? What do you know?"

"Rosie, I'm a newsman, and I'd be a fool to ask anyone to partner with me if I didn't know anything about them. To begin with, all you have to do is Google your name. You come up as a graduate of Cornell with a degree in English literature and a minor in finance. You also have a degree from the School of Metaphysics. You write for *Women Living Well* magazine with a body/mind/spirit column. Do you want me to go on?"

"Wow, I guess you know your stuff, all right," I said, impressed. "I want you to know I also Googled you. You graduated from USC with a degree in English literature and a minor in international business. You then got a BA from Ashford in social and criminal justice, which I find interesting."

"I'm impressed too. Glad you did some homework."

"Now, let me ask you a personal question, if I may. Who is the person who broke your heart?"

His face froze with surprise, then fell. His eyes watered. "How do you know about that?"

"I don't really, but I see a broken heart whenever I think of you. Are you willing to tell me about that?"

His eyes continued to tear up, and I could see I had found his soft spot. He looked away, lost in his thoughts. After more than a minute of silence, he turned and faced me with an anguished expression. "To answer your question about the person who broke my heart—it's someone I cared for deeply."

"Oh, my. I'm so sorry. You don't have to say anymore if you don't want to."

"Well, I think you're probably right. We shouldn't hide anything from each other if we're to be partners in crime. No pun intended," he added with a crooked smile. I remained silent, knowing I already was doing just that—hiding things from him. He heaved a sigh. "It happened a long time ago …."

I had a quick vision of a young woman, her eyes dull and void, her body full of tears. I knew she was no longer alive; I could sense it had been his sister. I wondered whether he felt guilty, perhaps not unlike what I'd been going through with thoughts of Jeff. Angrily, he pushed his drink away. "I swore from that day forward …."

I placed my hand on his arm. Seeing the look on my face, he remained silent. I was mortified by what I'd heard and the vision I had. I knew whoever it was had endured a senseless death—senseless because of the lack of kindness and concern for a human being who had suffered at the hands of another. I looked at him, his eyes drilled into mine, and I felt my heart cracking. "Is that why you got your degree in social and criminal justice?" I asked.

I had my answer when he stared at me and didn't respond. I tried to lighten the mood and teased, "Does that mean that as partners, we're going to be like Batman and Robin?"

Brian looked surprised, then laughed out loud with a full belly laugh. "Thanks, I needed that. By the way, I didn't come to Las Vegas by chance. I transferred here to sign on with Channel 5 News. I have some unfinished business here. I knew this would be a good place to get my revenge," he said as he struck a villainous pose.

I felt a pang of remorse. I instinctively knew Brian had withheld information from me as I had from him. Perhaps I had met my match.

During our conversation, Brian ignored his phone ringing. When it began to ring again for the third time, he picked it up and listened to an excited voice speaking to him. I felt a swish of energy, and my heart sank. I knew without a doubt what had happened.

As Brian's face flushed with excitement, he pocketed his phone and turned to me. "There's been another murder. You're not going to believe who it is!"

"Sally Smith," I said with certainty.

He looked at me in surprise. "'You got some 'splaining to do, Lucy.'"

"You have no idea, Cowboy."

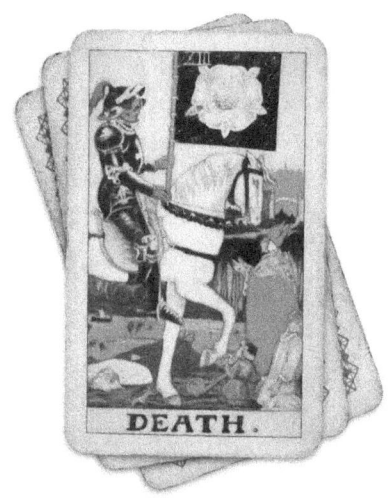

CHAPTER 7

Brian grabbed my hand, pulling me to his parked car around the corner of Sam's. He insisted we ride together. That turned into a scary car race as we dodged in and around other drivers, making me squeal in fright.

"Hold on tight, Rosie!" Brian hollered. "I don't want to miss the chance to be first at the crime scene. The station's already sent my cameraman to meet us there. I don't want to be late."

We arrived in no time, only to see Sally Smith's prone body carried out of an apartment building on a stretcher. Oddly, she lay there without a body bag, almost as if they had been in a hurry to get her out of there. The blanket covering her body slipped, and you didn't have to be close to see that her throat had been slit and was covered in blood. As I took in the expression of fear frozen on her face, I felt faint and had to squat down. My lord, what is happening? And why?

Brian's camera crew had set up the lights and the paraphernalia in record time, making him the first reporter on the scene. He was in his glory. He began reporting this very disturbing murder, the second within a week. I stood far from him. I didn't want to appear as part of the reporting crew in any way. A crowd had gathered, and I disappeared into it.

"Well," some lady puffed, "this is what happens when you show off your body like she did, parading her stuff through town. Not to mention being a part of the sordid happenings at that disgusting club."

"Oh, Gertie," her friend implored. "No one deserves this."

A man pushed through the crowd, heading toward the building and demanding, "Outta my way." I didn't recognize him, although his demanding voice sounded familiar. Something about him disturbed me. Who was he? Was he another newsman? That old feeling of danger gnawed at my innards.

I turned to the person beside me and asked, "Who's that man? Do you know his name?"

The man standing next to me looked at me oddly. "What man?"

"The man who just pushed by us!"

"I don't know what you're talking about, lady. No one came through here!"

I realized that it was happening again. A realistic premonition. "So sorry. Guess I was mistaken."

As I closed my eyes, another vision of the man I had just seen came to me. He was fiercely arguing with another man. It appeared he was threatening him. Who was he?

"Rosie, are you ready to go?" asked Brian. He was standing over me with a curious look. "Are you okay? You're white as a sheet."

"Sure thing," I responded, knowing more trouble was brewing. A headache was gathering strength. Goose bumps covered my body, a sure sign that my hunch would become a reality. I was too tired to think straight. I asked Brian, "Would you mind dropping me off at home? I'll pick my car up tomorrow."

Brian was pumped up by the excitement of his reporting and all that was happening. "Not so fast. We still need to talk, remember?"

I groaned but realized he was right. "Okay. I'll make some coffee, and then we can talk."

When we arrived at the house, Sweet Pea went crazy with excitement to see Brian again. He seemed thrilled with all her attention. It interested me that my cute little dog could quickly turn into a twirling ball of fur when any man was around, but I didn't want to spoil Brian's good fun by telling him that.

After Sweet Pea settled down next to Brian on the couch, I began to tell Brian everything I knew about Melissa and the meeting with Sally Smith—everything but the money part. I don't know why I didn't say anything, but I felt I was not supposed to reveal that to anyone.

It was late, and we both were exhausted. We'd have to wait and see what tomorrow would bring. I cleared the coffee cups, taking them into the kitchen. By the time I returned, Brian was asleep on the couch, with Sweet Pea curled up next to him. I decided to let him stay where he was, something so foreign to me that I amazed myself. Without another thought, I grabbed the throw from the back of the couch, placed it around Brian, picked up Sweet Pea, and headed upstairs to bed.

CHAPTER 8

F or once, I slept through the night without needing to get up. At our regular wake-up time in the morning, Sweet Pea licked my face and pranced around on the bed, but then she must have realized that her newfound playmate was still downstairs. Before I could grab her, she bounded down the wooden stairs, with her toenails clicking their tune on the way down. I pulled on my pink cashmere robe I always threw across the boudoir chair close to the bed and hurried after her. I heard Brian's laughter before I reached the bottom of the stairs.

"Hey, there. Oh, nooo, stop. You're tickling me!" His laughter was contagious. I chuckled with him as Sweet Pea jumped on his stomach, trying to reach his cheek to give him good-morning licks.

"Good morning, Cowboy," I called out. I left them alone and went into the kitchen to start the coffee.

A few minutes later, Brian entered the kitchen and sat on one of the counter stools. I appreciated that he seemed subdued and not flirtatious, for I had no intention of getting romantically involved with him or any man. He greeted me with a crooked smile.

After I handed him a cup of coffee, he suggested, "Let's plan out what each of us can do today to see what we can find out. How about you see what you can find out about Melissa, and I'll follow the trail with Sally Smith."

Just like a man, I thought. Go for the big boobs. As if he could read my mind, he added, "Melissa for you since you knew her best, right?"

I nodded and asked, "Do you have time for some breakfast?"

"Oh, shit!" he exclaimed as he looked at his watch. "I've got to run and get to the office. I'll call you later. You've got my cell phone number, right?"

He turned away before I could answer. "Good luck!" I called to his retreating back.

"Right on!" he responded, and he was gone.

Unhappy to have him leave, Sweet Pea looked at me accusingly as if I had said something to chase him off. I ignored her, and with another cup of coffee, I went to the patio to plan my day.

It would be a good day to call Melissa's mother with my condolences and see whether I could help her in any way. It would probably be a good idea to contact Melissa's roommate. Before I contacted either one, I wanted to fully understand more of a stripper's life and the world she lived in. Thinking I would get answers from Google more quickly than reading chapters in "The Las Vegas Madame," I turned to my computer. I'd read the book later.

I love my computer! It has so much information right at hand. Gone are the days of going to the library, trying to find and gather the information I wanted, which was usually spread throughout several books and took a lot of time to assemble.

When I was younger, mentioning a stripper automatically turned my thoughts to Gypsy Rose Lee, the American burlesque entertainer famous for her striptease act. I found it intriguing that while Gypsy Rose Lee was stripping, her sister was the renowned actress June Havoc. What a captivating pair!

But what continued to fascinate me was that Gypsy Rose Lee gained respect not only as a striptease artist but also as an accomplished actress. In addition, she became an author and playwright whose 1957 memoir was made into the stage musical and film "Gypsy."

So when did a striptease artist become known as a lap dancer or exotic dancer rather than someone with the more classy title of performer? As I began reading one site, the image of the strippers we know today evolved through the 1960s and 1970s. By the 1980s, pole dancing and its highly expressive style became widely accepted and frequently portrayed in film, television, and theater.

Knowing that Melissa wanted to escape her circumstances, I felt for her. But where did all that money stuffed in her envelope come from?

I wasn't sure what Melissa's mother could share with me. I knew I had to tread lightly, for most dancers' parents aren't too happy with their children's choices. I remembered Melissa's note, which had her mother's address in South Bend, Indiana. I also remembered that her mother's last name wasn't Johnson but Givens. I Googled her name and remembered her address, School Street, by a stroke of luck.

There it was—her telephone number from the white pages software program for South Bend. "Lord, there is no such thing as privacy anymore, is there?" I mumbled.

I picked up my cell phone and dialed Mrs. Givens' number. After three rings, I was pleasantly surprised to hear a sweet, somewhat frail voice.

"Hello? Is this Mrs. Givens?"

"Yes, it is. Who are you?"

"My name is Rosalie Bennett. I knew your daughter. I wanted to pay my condolences for your loss and to say I'm so sorry for Melissa's death. Is there anything I can do for you?"

"What can you do for me now? It's a little late for that," she sniffed.

"I was wondering if you will be coming to Las Vegas soon. Are you planning to have some service for Melissa?"

At this, Melissa's mother began to cry. "N...n...no. The police won't release her body yet. They told me that under the circumstances, it'd be better if I had her body cremated once they released it. They told me not to bother to come right now." She sniffled some more. "They offered to save me the trouble of coming at all. They'd be happy to send me her ashes after everything had been taken care of."

I found that extremely strange. When did the police department become involved in funerals for murder victims?

"Do you need me to check on anything for you? Would you like me to gather whatever items the police didn't remove and send them to you? Would that help you?"

I heard a slight pause in her sniffling, and then she spoke. "That will be lovely, dear. What did you say your name was again?"

"Rosalie Bennett. I'm a friend of Melissa, remember?"

"I'm sorry. Yes, of course. You sounded like the other girl who called and asked me all those questions. My mind is muddled. So much has happened in the past few days."

"Mrs. Givens, was the other girl who called you Melissa's roommate?"

"I don't think so. I think she said her name was Sally. But she wasn't making much sense. She kept asking me if I'd received a package from Melissa and if I would help her. She said she was in trouble. I didn't know what she was talking about."

"I wonder how she knew where to contact you."

"The same way you did, I suppose. Melissa."

That didn't make sense to me. At the time of her reading, Melissa told me that she didn't let anyone know where she grew up or anything about her background. She wasn't about to either, she'd said. She didn't want her mother to realize what she was doing in Las Vegas—stripping. I hadn't thought much of it then, for I believed many dancers probably felt the same way. And didn't the girls have an unspoken pact not to rat on each other? So what was up with Sally? What had she said to Melissa's mother?

Before saying goodbye to Melissa's mother on my cell phone, I promised to contact her soon. I turned from my computer and spotted my outdated office phone. It was partially hidden underneath a pile of papers I had thrown onto the back corner of my desk. I felt goosebumps as I removed the documents and saw a blinking red light indicating a voicemail message. I already knew whose it was. I was stricken by the fact that it was too late to help.

When I pushed the button, the phone automatically announced the date and time of the voicemail. It had come in at 5:20 p. m. the day before when I was on my way to meet Brian at Sam's Roadhouse. I listened to Sally's frantic voice—"Rosalie, you've got to help me, please! They think I know where to find whatever Melissa stole from them, but I don't. They're going to kill me. Call me, please!" Noises entered the line for a second or two before all went silent.

My hands started to shake; I first felt hot, then cold. Had I told Sally I had the money, could I have saved her life? Why was I holding back from letting anyone know about the money? Each time I thought I should report it, I sensed a NO. Why? I reached for the stuffed chair in my office and collapsed onto it. What had I done?

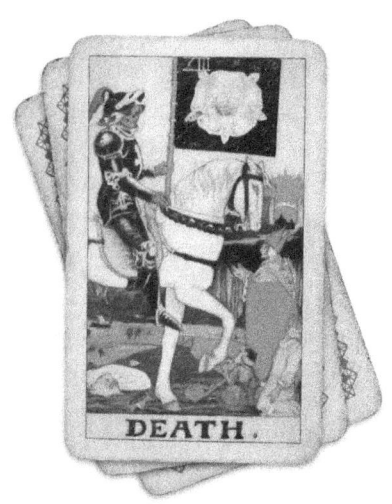

CHAPTER 9

I knew I should call Brian to confess my part in the murders. Before I did, though, I was prompted to look at Melissa's envelope again. Something wasn't adding up in that two murders had been committed for $23,345. Nothing to sniff at, but still ….

I went upstairs, shut my bedroom door, and went to my secret hiding place to pull out Melissa's package. I turned the package upside down and dumped out the money, the note to me, and the letter Melissa had left for her mother. I picked up the letter and decided I'd gone this far, so I might as well read it for clues as to what was going on.

"Dear Mom, I'm sorry for all the trouble I have caused you. Yes, I agree it is time to come home …" There were more personal messages that I was uncomfortable reading. No clues there, so I concentrated on counting out the money again. $23,305! Something was wrong—I was off by $40.

I'm very accurate at counting money or doing sums. My heart began to beat wildly. That couldn't be. Calm down, I said to myself. The other cash must still be in the envelope. I picked it up, holding it upside down again, and shook it. Nothing came out. Odd. I peeked inside and could see the bills. They were stuck on something. I opened the large envelope wider and saw torn pages from a small notebook taped inside.

I pulled the pages out, and two $20 bills dropped to the floor. I saw a note taped to them that had caused all three to stick to the inside. Unease came over me when I saw a second note addressed to me! "If you are reading this, I am probably dead, and you are in danger just because you have these in hand. Although they don't mean anything to you because they are in code, they mean a great deal to the person who will be destroyed if this information gets out. I took these as insurance so no one would hurt my family or me. Do with them what you will. I'm sorry."

My head was pounding in sync with my heartbeat. I wasn't even sure whom I could turn to or whom to trust. Even Brian. I needed a break from all of this. I packed everything, including the letter to Melissa's mom, back into the envelope, then stuffed it into my safekeeping spot. After I saw which of Melissa's things I could collect and return to her mother, I'd slip the letter into the mix.

I was beside myself with worry. There was only one way to lessen my stress. As ridiculous as it might have seemed, I knew what would help me—shopping. Besides, I needed to replace the tired, worn-out black boots I loved, which I found hard to part with. Now was a good time to replace them, especially with the fabulous sales on last season's boots.

It was a peaceful retreat. Oddly, Sweet Pea didn't seem to care about joining me. It's easy for me to relax when I shop because I don't think about my worries; I'm simply on the hunt for whatever I need. If I had tried on one pair of boots, I must have tried on 20! I purchased a tall, black leather pair and a short, black suede pair. I was triumphant to have gotten both pairs of boots at a super sale price, and my spirits lifted.

I happily burst through the garage door at home, lugging my packages. As soon as I opened the door, I found Sweet Pea right there to greet me. Strange. She wasn't wiggling around, welcoming me as usual. Instead, she stared deeply into my eyes, trying to tell me something. She walked to the front hall closet and stood before it, wagging her tail. She looked at me without barking, which was even stranger. As goosebumps crawled along my body, I realized someone must be inside that closet.

I called out in a loud voice, "Sweet Pea, you need to go out. C'mon, potty time." Just as I swooped down to pick her up and make our escape, someone crashed through the closet door. He pushed me to the floor, hitting my head in the process. Before I could regroup to see who it was, he'd exited. I struggled to get up onto my knees, which was particularly difficult because Sweet Pea was on top of me, licking my face. What to do next?

Since I wasn't injured, first things first. I went into my office and wasn't surprised to see everything torn apart. As I put it all back in order, my heart sank. I wasn't sure what this was going to mean for me.

I knew it was time to call Brian and tell him what had happened. I still had no intention of telling him about Melissa's package and what was in it. What he didn't know couldn't hurt him. After all, there was no use putting him in danger too.

Brian didn't answer his cell phone, so I left a message for him to call me when he could. Then I placed a call to Melissa's roommate, Mary.

The telephone rang and rang with no answer. I began to panic, thinking perhaps there'd been another murder. Suddenly, I heard a drowsy voice say, "Yesss, who's this? What do you want?"

"Hi, Mary. This is Rosalie Bennett. I'm helping Melissa's mother get some of Melissa's things from the apartment to send to her. Is there a time that works for you when we can get together?"

"Not right now. I'm not even awake yet. What time is it anyway?"

"It's 1:30 in the afternoon."

"Wow, I'm sleeping in late for sure. Let's see, how about 4 o'clock to meet?"

"Sure. That works for me. What's the address?"

After giving me the address, Mary hung up, and I stood still. I wondered about the next best thing for me to do until 4. I needed to sit down and organize in my head the events that had taken place since I first met Melissa.

"Gram, this is a mess! What am I going to do now?" I implored her, not expecting an answer.

She surprised me. "Rosie girl, I wish I could interfere but can't. Just follow your heart."

"Great," I mumbled. "Since when do you not interfere?" As I felt her shaking her head at me, I said, "Sorry, Gram. I know you're right. I have to figure out this mess as soon as I can."

I heard her parting words floating in the air. "I can tell you that things aren't what they seem." And then, poof! She was gone once again, showing me a red rose for love.

I began my list of events concerning Melissa from when we first sat across from each other that fateful day, which now seemed ages ago.

1. Melissa, a dancer at the Purple Passion Club—who was her boss?
2. Melissa's new job driving for PUP—why there?
3. Melissa with a black eye—who hit her?
4. Melissa's package and leaving Las Vegas—what had changed her mind?
5. Melissa beaten and murdered—done by the same person who gave her the black eye?
6. Meeting Sally—did she know about coded papers?
7. Who was the man with Sally?
8. Missed a phone call from Sally and the frantic voicemail—what was the connection between Sally and Melissa, if any?
9. What does the roommate know about both Melissa and Sally?

The phone rang; it was Brian calling. After I picked up, I heard him say, "Hi, Rosie, what's happening?"

Upon hearing his voice, I immediately burst into tears of relief, surprising us both.

"What's going on, Rosie? What's wrong? Are you okay?"

I sniffled, saying, "My goodness, I don't know where that came from. Yes, of course, I'm okay; nothing to worry about. I just had a little upset here at the house. Someone broke in and was hiding in the hall closet. He rushed out of here, knocking me down, and took off."

"My gosh! Are you hurt? Why would anyone break into your house? What were they looking for, do you know?" he asked, worry in his voice.

"I don't know," I lied. "He tore through my office, but I couldn't find anything missing when I put everything back together."

"Rosie, what are you hiding from me?" he demanded.

What was the matter with me that I couldn't tell him the truth? Keeping secrets like this was against everything I believed in, especially if we were indeed partners in crime. Nothing good was going to come of this, I knew. And yet … I held back.

"Rosie, are you there?"

"Yes, I'm here."

"I have to go on air in about five minutes. Turn on the news for an update. Call me if anything else happens, hear?" Brian said in a rush.

I turned on the television and sat on the couch, waiting for the 3 o'clock news. There he was, looking professional and stern.

"This is Brian Boyce, Channel 5 News, reporting an update on the two murders within the past week."

The screen flashed to an announcement from the Chief of Police. "We are investigating these crimes as two separate events. We do not believe these deaths are related, even though both girls were known as exotic entertainers in the downtown area."

I was furious. The Chief of Police made it sound like Melissa's and Sally's murders were caused by choosing exotic dancing as a career.

Brian showed up on the screen, standing close to the Chief of Police and asking him, "Are you saying that nothing more is going to be done to see whether they are connected?"

The Chief of Police shot daggers at Brian. "Of course not," he snapped. "This will continue to be an ongoing investigation for each of them. Sometimes in such cases, it takes time to follow up on leads because the victims have been exposed to so many people, as I am sure *you* must realize." In a cold voice, he continued, "We'll inform the public as information becomes available. Thank you."

"And so you have it. Brian Boyce, Channel 5 News. Over and out."

My heart was pounding as I watched the Chief of Police and heard what he had to say. He was the same arrogant man who had denied me an autopsy for Jeff. I despised him. No wonder I didn't want to get involved with the police. They couldn't be trusted.

Things had a way of coming full circle. Maybe, the Chief of Police would get the comeuppance I believed he deserved. I, for one, would be glad to see that happen to him. Besides, right now, I told myself, you have better things to do this minute than waste your thoughts on a man like him. It was time to meet Mary at the apartment, so I hurriedly gathered some large trash bags and a few boxes to pack whatever I needed to return to Melissa's mother. I said goodbye to Sweet Pea and headed out. I was curious to hear what Mary would tell me.

J.S. Peck

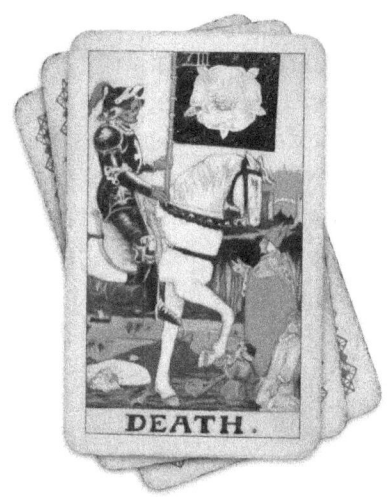

CHAPTER 10

Mary greeted me warmly. "Hey, Rosalie. How are you doing? Come on in." She seemed more subdued and less provocative than on television—less "on stage."

She took me on a tour of the condo before she led me to the couch in the large living room, which had a small deck attached. The condo was nicely laid out, with two separate master bedroom suites, a nice-sized dining room, and a great kitchen with stainless steel appliances and a center island. Other than a few of Mary's clothes strewn around, the condo was neat and clean.

As we sat down on the couch, Mary turned to me sadly. "Melissa confessed to me about her reading with you. She said that the Death card had come up, and she was worried about it. Did you know all of this was going to happen?"

"I hope Melissa mentioned the Death card doesn't necessarily mean death. It can stand for a new beginning, which we both know Melissa was doing with her new job at PUP," I answered, dodging her question.

Mary said nothing, just nodded her head. "She told me she had some business to handle but didn't say what."

"Did you tell the police about what she'd said or that she had a reading with me?"

"After all the harassment they give us, I wouldn't tell them squat. You should be wary of the police too. Some are dirty. It's just a fact of life."

I wondered how someone had connected me to Melissa and, because of that, broke into my house searching for what I now believed they wanted—Melissa's notes. Was it Mary? I would have to find a connection somewhere. For now, I changed the subject. "I'm curious. Why did she choose PUP for her next job?"

Mary laughed and said, "We thought the name was so cute. Later, she told me her boss had originally suggested it. He had even offered to help her find the perfect car for the job. As it turned out, he is the one who bought it for her."

"Why would her boss do that—suggest the job at PUP and get her the car?"

"Probably because he knew she was tired of dancing, but he wanted to keep her around. I think he had a crush on her. He's okay. It's the big bosses who are creeps. You know, the ones who run the club. I get the chills even thinking of them." Sure enough, she shivered and closed her arms around her.

"Mary, how did you and Melissa meet?"

"We started dancing together where I work now, but it was too sedate for Melissa—not enough tips. She liked the excitement of the Purple Passion Lounge. When she was offered the job there, she jumped at it. She was looking for another condo closer to her work and asked me if I'd be her roommate. So I said yes, and the rest is history."

When she realized she sounded flippant, Mary's eyes filled. "I miss her, even though we haven't spent much time together the past few weeks."

"Yes, I can see that you do. I'm so sorry."

Mary wiped a few tears away and was silent.

"Do you know if the club's bosses have anything to do with PUP?" I pushed.

"No idea, but I wouldn't be surprised if they do. I would be cautious around them. They have their fingers in a lot of pots. They're not nice guys."

"Why would Melissa even work there, then?"

"Everything was money to her. She planned to make as much money as possible and buy a little house for herself and her mother. She said her mother was older and would die if she found out what she was doing. Now, of course, everything will come out."

"Have you ever met her mother or talked to her on the phone?"

"Surprisingly, no. As I said, Melissa didn't want anyone to know she even had a mother. If you asked her about it, she'd tell you her mother died when she was little. I still don't think too many people know her mother is alive. I don't even know her full name or where she lives." She added, "It's interesting that the news people haven't picked up on it yet."

"Well, let's hope it stays that way," I said, worrying that someone might hurt Melissa's mother by trying to learn whether she had received a package from Melissa.

"Have the police been asking you a lot of questions about Melissa's family?"

"No, not of me. Strangely, I have talked to the police just once, and only briefly. I told them what I told the news people … that I don't know much about Melissa's new job or who may have wanted to hurt her. All my times and whereabouts are well documented. There's no reason for them to believe differently. I played dumb."

"It seems odd the police aren't being more aggressive in their search for the killer. It's almost as if the police treat this like another retaliation murder for a girl being a dancer. In other words, not worth much effort," I said with annoyance.

"We girls get that all the time. Believe me, being in this business, we learn pretty quickly to become bulletproof from everything said to humiliate us. I have no shame about what I do, especially when I compare myself and what I do with some business people in town who come into the club pulling their crap. Even some politicians are real jerks, thinking they are above the law too. And the code of courtesy? Forget it."

"Anyone in particular?" I asked.

"Not really. Take a good look around. You'd be surprised how many people in power abuse it in so many ways. They act so entitled; it's ridiculous."

Thinking about the money Melissa had stashed in the envelope, I asked, "Does the Purple Passion Lounge pay that much more than what she was earning at your place?"

"Every place can be a little bit different. We don't make as much as escorts, who can be on their own without the hassle of being snubbed by the other dancers. We have to pay the house fee and tip the valet, the DJ, the house "mom," waitresses, bartenders, and bouncers. Sometimes, you can make a special deal with the boss if you are outstanding. I think that's what Melissa did, but I'm unsure."

I looked at my watch and couldn't believe 40 minutes had passed! "Oh, Mary! I'm so sorry for taking up so much of your time! I'd better collect Melissa's things and let you return to what you were doing."

"No problem, Rosalie. Melissa told me there is something about you that gave her courage. She said she trusted you. I know you want to find out who did this to Melissa as much as I do."

"I do," I responded.

"And Sally Smith, too," she added. "Sally? Did you know her?" I asked.

"Not really, but she's still one of us. Melissa knew her, though, since they worked together at the lounge."

It was interesting that there seemed to be some genuine caring about another "sister" in the business. A good thing to remember.

Mary and I sorted through Melissa's things, though there weren't many other things besides her clothes. Since Mary and Melissa wore the same size, we decided that Mary could pick the clothing she wanted. Anything she didn't like, she would give to Goodwill.

We found a small black box underneath her panties and bras containing a beautiful diamond ring. With it was a card with the words "You are the one. Love, B.B." The first name that came to mind was Brian Boyce, which was ridiculous. However, his having the same initials as Brian would make it easier for me to remember them. "Oh, my!" I exclaimed, "What a beautiful ring."

"Wow, I didn't know that was there," Mary said in amazement.

"Do you know who B.B. is?"

"Gosh, I don't. As I said, Melissa and I kinda went separate ways the last month or so. Even our schedules didn't match up. Lately, when I'd enter the living room, and Melissa was on the phone, she'd hang up quickly without saying much more than goodbye."

"What should we do about the ring?" Mary asked. "Do you think someone will come looking for it?"

"I'm not sure," I answered with increasing concern.

"Well, I've had enough trauma. I'm leaving to return home tomorrow or the next day for a new start, so you'll have to take it."

Worry came over me as I took the ring, two small boxes of Melissa's things, primarily books, a few photos I had hurriedly grabbed from her bookcase, and a box of lovely but inexpensive costume jewelry. I thanked Mary, wished her luck, and headed home.

My mind was whirling with so many thoughts. I kept thinking of the vision I had seen at the site of Sally's death. I wondered who the man was, for he seemed vaguely familiar. He had been rude and uncaring as his energy pushed through the crowd. I did not doubt that he had something to do with Sally's death.

My head was beginning to pound thinking of what I had read—the rate of sexual abuse in the past 20 years was the highest it had ever been. And truth be told, the abuse of men by women was increasingly countering the mistreatment of women by men. I have learned that their need for control increases when people feel out of control. I knew that was true for me. I realized that murders are simply the overpowering of the victim to gain control of something real or imagined in the murderer's mind. A power struggle? Is that what it had boiled down to for Melissa and Sally?

Death on the Strip

I was beginning to understand why Sarah and her *Women Living Well* magazine staff were so excited about starting their transformation. It was partly because there were so many different angles to consider. Taking part in that would not be as simple a task as I'd thought, especially since I'd kept my life sheltered from the real world on many levels for the past few years. I very rarely watched the news, as I didn't want any of that negative energy around me. Am I ready to jump in and do that? I asked myself. "Darn right I am," I responded in a loud, determined voice.

It was time for me to step forward. More than anything, I wanted Melissa's and Sally's murders solved, and I wouldn't rest until they were.

CHAPTER 11

At home, I walked through the door, greeted Sweet Pea with a treat, and poured myself a glass of wine. I collapsed on the couch, exhausted. I could hear my cell phone ringing and ignored it. I needed time to regroup and was unaware my eyes had closed in sleep.

I woke up about an hour later. I hauled the two boxes of Melissa's things from my car and tucked them into my garage to mail to her mother another day. I took the box with the diamond ring out of my purse and put it in my bedroom's safekeeping spot. As I was doing so, I heard Sweet Pea barking in delight. I got goosebumps. It had to be Brian, and for reasons I couldn't explain, I was both unenthusiastic yet glad he was here. Maybe he had something new to report.

He greeted me with a grin when I opened the door for him. "I called you earlier. I hope I'm not interrupting anything."

"No, not really."

"So, Rosie, anything new?"

"Actually, something very interesting." Sweet Pea was beside herself to see him, blocking Brian from entering. "Sweet Pea," I said, "Stop jumping around and let him in."

"Come on, girl," he said to the dog as he entered, heading for the couch in the living room. "Do you have a cup of coffee for a tired reporter, Rosie girl?"

"Sure," I responded. I looked back to see Brian patting the space next to him on the couch, making room for Sweet Pea. I thought you've got to love any guy for that alone, even if I'm not interested in him.

I fixed the coffee, made a chicken sandwich for each of us, and joined him in the living room. After he finished eating, he said, "Okay, Detective Rosie. Let 'er rip. What's the news?"

I had given careful thought to what I would divulge. I was not going to say anything about the diamond ring just yet; the timing wasn't right. So I said, "According to Melissa's roommate, Mary, Melissa's boss had suggested she work at PUP. He's also the person who bought the car for her to drive. Something's got to be up with that, right?"

He looked surprised and wrote that information down in a small notepad he pulled from his shirt pocket.

"Mary also said she's had only one short visit from the police asking her questions. Don't you find that odd? Don't you think they'd be more aggressive in questioning her? After all, she's the one who lived with Melissa. Get this—their condo hasn't even been searched! When I asked Mary about it, she said the police were sending someone over tomorrow to go through the condo. It seems the police aren't doing much to find Melissa's killer. What do you think?"

"I agree. Whenever I tell my boss I'd like to follow up with the police, he says, 'Don't bother. They're doing all they can. They'll let us know when there's an update.' I think that's a bit strange too."

"What did you find out about Sally?" I asked, curious to know what he'd discovered.

"She lived alone in the apartment building where we were the other night. No eyewitnesses have come forward, although one older lady I spoke with on the night of the murder thought she heard skirmishes. I don't think she's reliable, though, so no real leads yet. I'll follow up with the old lady when I can."

"I haven't been able to talk to Melissa's big boss or anyone at the Purple Passion Lounge. It seems they aren't talking to anyone but the police. However, there must be some connection between the boss and Sally. She was the only one used for billboard advertising. That's a bit unusual, I think. According to one of the girls who works there, Sally was given special treatment. All the girls were miffed about it. "

"I wondered about that," I added, "especially since Sally was not especially beautiful compared to Melissa— and I imagine some other girls there too."

"I agree," Brian said, nodding his head.

After a pause, he said, "Rosie, I've been thinking about a plan that I think can get us the information we want. Want to hear it?" he asked hesitantly.

"Okay," I responded, not sure I would like it. It almost seemed like child's play, but I reminded myself to stay open and listen to what Brian had to offer. In all the time I worked with the police on various cases, I'd never worked one in such an unorthodox way.

"I think you should apply to be one of the girls at the Purple Passion Lounge. You're pretty enough, and you have a great figure. You'd be a shoo-in."

"What are you thinking I'd be doing there?" I asked in a frosty tone, strangely annoyed by his "pretty enough" comment.

"Gathering information, of course," he returned with a slight grin.

"Well, I have a better idea, mister. You go to the club. As a client, I'm sure you won't have any trouble getting the girls to talk. You may even be 'pretty enough' in the looks department too." I added sweetly. "And what had you in mind for what you'd be doing while I was at the lounge?"

"I thought I could become a part-time driver for PUP," he responded. Seeing my disbelief, he asked, "Why? Would you rather do that?"

"Of course, I'd rather be a driver than a stripper," I responded with dignity, realizing too late that I had fallen into his trap.

After soaking up what had just happened and being annoyed by my stupidity, I snapped, "For God's sake, Sweet Pea, stop mauling him with all your kisses and get down off the couch."

As Brian started to open his mouth in protest, I barked at him, "Don't even think about it, Cowboy."

He promptly closed his mouth. He realized he had pushed his luck far enough by getting me to commit to driving for PUP. He hurriedly got up from the couch and headed for the front door. I followed. When he reached it, he turned to me, kissed my forehead, and said, "I'll be back tomorrow in time for a morning cup of coffee, okay? We can begin to put our plans into action then."

As Sweet Pea looked forlornly at the front door, I said, "And you! Don't even think about giving me a dirty look, Missy! C'mon, we're going to bed."

Then I remembered I had forgotten to have Brian listen to Sally's message. I intended to do so before we discussed who would do what between PUP and the Purple Passion Lounge. I was so surprised yet annoyed by my reactions to Brian that I was happy to put myself to bed and forget my foolish behavior. He certainly knew how to get under my skin.

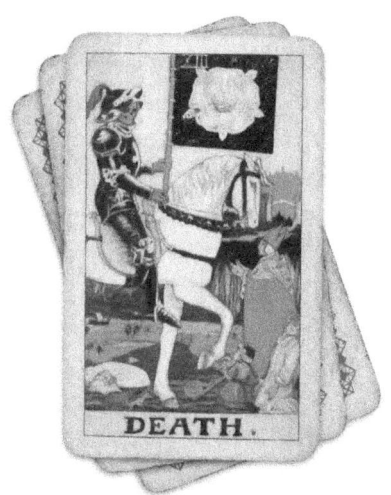

CHAPTER 12

I t was no surprise that I tossed and turned during the night and woke up grumpy. I smelled the perfume my grandmother always wore, and I wasn't surprised to hear her whispering, "Remember, Sunshine, if you don't get up on the right side of the bed, that is how your whole day will be. Why don't you take a few minutes and start over?" She sent me a vision of a red rose for love and puff; she was gone.

I lay in bed, trying to regain a better frame of mind. I had to smile about Gram's coming to me. Even all these years later, she still treated me as her little girl who needed her guidance occasionally. I knew how important it was not to give your power away to please someone else. I needed to be sure that driving part-time for PUP was a good thing for me to do. I also needed to rethink my relationship with Brian. What did I really know about him?

I got up, showered, and dressed before I headed downstairs for a cup of morning coffee. I let Sweet Pea out, and then I sat before my computer. PUP's website had a place to download an application, which I filled out and returned to them via email. I printed out a copy for myself as well. I planned on hand-delivering it to them that day, so I used MapQuest to find their address.

I had finished when I heard Sweet Pea barking excitingly, so I knew Brian was there. When I opened the door and saw him, I couldn't help exclaiming, "Whoa, Cowboy, what happened to you? You look awful!"

He answered grumpily, "After I left you last night, I thought there was no reason to delay going to the Purple Passion Lounge. Let me tell you, that place is hoppin'. I didn't get home until four this morning."

"Good lord! What did you do there all that time?"

He gave his crooked grin, "What do you think?"

I hate it when anyone does that, leaving me with nothing witty to say. "Well?" I asked, ignoring his question.

He laughed. "Well, I got to know two of the girls pretty well," he said with a wink.

I couldn't help being annoyed by his inferences. "I don't care about that. Come on, what did they *say*?"

All business now, he replied, "Actually, they told me quite a lot. Melissa's supervisor is David Masterly, and. Her death broke him up. In fact, he hasn't been back in the office since she died. The girls said his wife arranged for them to take some time off these past few days in Hawaii. They say the wife is a tough cookie and unpleasant and that he'd be better off working than spending time with her no matter how beautiful a place is."

"Two partners own the business. One is a silent partner, and no one knows who it is. The partner who runs the business is Tony Angelo. He can be a prick, according to the girls. David is in charge of all the girls, and everyone I spoke to says he is a really nice guy who ensured everything went as smoothly as possible. He was a bit sweet on Melissa, but they think it was probably more like a fatherly love. He's quite a bit older than she was."

"Hmmm. Maybe that's why David helped Melissa get her car for a new start in life," I interjected. "What about Sally Smith?"

"There is some connection between Tony and Sally, but no one knows exactly what it is. The girls say Sally was nice enough but acted more like a puppet for Tony. Whatever she wanted, she got. Melissa and Sally got along okay but weren't close.

"I haven't been able to talk to Tony, but I will go there later today to see what I can find out. Meanwhile, I'll check with the station to see if they have anything on him that isn't public information."

"How about you, Sunshine?" Brian asked.

Brian's question startled me, for Sunshine was the name my grandmother had used this morning. I found it odd, too, that both of them sometimes called me "Rosie girl." Strange.

I couldn't let go of my curiosity about the diamond ring with the signature of B.B. that Mary and I had discovered in Melissa's things. Although it didn't seem likely that the ring was from Brian, I had to know it wasn't. "I told you about the diamond ring Mary and I found among Melissa's things, didn't I?" I asked.

"No, what ring?" Brian asked with raised eyebrows.

"When we went through Melissa's things, we found a fancy jewelry box with a large diamond ring. There was also a note. It read, 'You are the one. Love, B.B.' Do you know anything about that?"

As I stared intently at Brian, his face flushed, and he looked flustered. I felt a flutter of worry in my stomach. I continued staring at him until he opened his eyes wide and held his hands up in defense. "You don't think it's me, do you? Well, it's not me!" he protested.

"Then why are you looking like a cat that has swallowed a canary?" I demanded.

"No reason." He replied uncomfortably before adding, "It's not me!"

I hurried to change the subject so he wouldn't ask where the ring was. "Well, then. Here's what else is happening. This morning, I got up and filled out an application for PUP and emailed it to them. I also printed one out for myself. I'll hand-deliver it there today. Perhaps I can even get them to interview me then," I said hopefully.

"Good," acknowledged Brian, happy to change the subject from the initials B. B. I wondered what that was all about. He asked, "By the way, do you have a whiteboard? I thought with all your writing, you might have one."

"Well, you're lucky because I have one in my office. Follow me."

"Wow, your office is so neat! How do you do it? I never can. I have things strewn all over the place. However, I pretty much know where everything is," he added. "Maybe I wouldn't if everything were this neat!"

I ignored his teasing. "Let me find the erasable pens, and we can start," I said excitedly. I remembered some of the scenes from the various television crime shows and how they worked with their whiteboards, unlike how Gram and I had done our police work by meditation when we were asked to help them psychically. "I'll put Melissa's name on the top left and Sally's on the top right."

As I began writing, I heard him say, "I believe there is a unique connection between the two that may not be obvious at first. But once we find out how they are connected, maybe we can get to the bottom of who the killer is."

"I agree," I said.

"Let's write under each name the things we know about them so far," suggested Brian.

I kept silent about what I was hiding from him. I was hoping Brian would discover some new information without my revealing what I was keeping to myself. Why was I not sharing what I knew about Melissa's money and codebook with him? What was holding me silent? All I could do was shake my head at myself and go along with my intuition, which was telling me to keep still.

With my heart pounding, I realized it was time to have Brian listen to Sally's message. I dreaded his reaction. "Brian, I was going to share something with you last night but lost track with all the talk about PUP and the Purple Passion Lounge. Please don't be upset with me. Just listen to this message, okay?"

"I knew you were hiding something," he scowled.

"Remember I told you about meeting Sally Smith?"

"Yeah," he nodded reluctantly.

"Yesterday morning, I discovered the message light blinking on the desk telephone. I'd hidden it underneath a newspaper I'd tossed in the corner. I need you to listen to it now."

My eyes watered, and I got goosebumps. As I listened to Sally's words again, I watched Brian's startled expression.

For once, he was silent, with no quick comeback. After a few long seconds, he turned to me. "Holy shit, Rosie."

"Do we have to report it to the police?" I asked with a silent, desperate plea for him to say no.

"Normally, I would say we have to, but for obvious reasons, I think if we do that, it's only going to make things worse for both of us, especially because we're investigating her murder, too." Brian seemed shaken by Sally's message. "Damn it! You aren't hiding anything else from me, are you?"

I turned away from him so I wouldn't have to look him in the eye, and I shook my head no. I reached for one of the pens for the whiteboard and suggested, "Let's list motives for both killings and see where that gets us."

"All right," Brian said, more enthused now that I was serious about helping him, but I could see he was still upset with me. It seemed that the tables had turned. It was now he who had doubts about why we were working together. I was trouble for him.

As I began writing—money/greed, revenge, jealousy, sex, recognition/fame, self-protection of personal status or loved one, rage, mental illness—I felt goosebumps. Again I remembered my vision when we went to Sally's murder scene.

"Did I forget anything?"

"The most important thing of all in my book is love," he said, looking at me with such innocence that my heart skipped a beat.

"I agree," I said with a nod. "Let's work it from that angle, then."

Once again, Brian became all business. He took over the board. "All right, we know there is a connection between

Melissa and Sally simply because they both worked at the Purple Passion Lounge. But what else?"

"I don't think that means very much. I think you're right. It has much more to do with their love lives and the men in them."

I thought of when I'd met Brian and asked, "By the way, did you know Melissa before she drove us to the airport that day when we first met?"

Brian looked surprised. "What do you mean?"

"That was the day I booked PUP for my airport pickup. According to the PUP rules I read this morning, the driver is allowed only one pickup. You were already in the car when she came to get me. Afterward, she said not to mention to anyone that she had two different pickups simultaneously."

"Oh, that." He answered, avoiding my question. "Nothing to worry about, Rosie."

"Just what kind of answer is that?" I pressed.

The look on Brian's face was an embarrassment. He gave a crooked smile. "I was at the same coffee shop when Melissa picked up her latte. I overheard her on her cell phone saying she'd be able to make the PUP trip to the airport, so in my charming way, I told her I had an emergency and had to get to the airport fast. I convinced her I would make it worthwhile if she ditched you and took me instead."

"You dirty dog!" I exclaimed, appalled.

"Well, as you know, she refused to dump you, so she got both my money and yours."

"And well deserved, if you ask me. Shame on you. Now I understand why you didn't want to say anything."

"I know. Later I felt bad that I had pushed Melissa into taking me to the airport. I never got the chance to tell her how sorry I was," he lamented.

I felt slightly sorry for him because it's so easy to let an apology lapse. We always think we have enough time to do so. When the phone rang, it startled me. Uncertain about who would be calling, I hesitated to pick it up. I looked at Brian, who lifted his shoulders, signaling he had no idea who the caller might be. So I gingerly picked up the phone. "Hello?"

"Is this Rosalie Bennett?" asked the voice on the phone.

"Yes. How may I help you?"

"Perhaps it's me who is going to help you! This is Sophia from PUP calling. We received your application this morning and would like to speak with you. Are you available this afternoon?"

CHAPTER 13

I closed the front door after pushing Brian out and raced to change my clothes to get to the PUP office. I was alarmed to discover its office in a rather seedy part of Las Vegas' early business center, which had gone to ruin.

I arrived right on time. When I went to open the door to the office, I found it unlocked. When I stepped inside, there was no one in the reception area. Before I could call out, I heard rumbling that sounded like furniture being moved coming from the back. The loud, demanding voice yelling at some unfortunate person froze me in my spot.

"What do you mean you don't know?" It was the voice I heard when I first called PUP. And, now, I recognized it as the same voice I had heard in my vision at Sally's death site.

I yelled as loudly as I could, "Anybody here?" I heard more shuffling, and a door slammed shut as a pretty older woman came rushing from the back. She looked under duress and more than a little disheveled.

"Hi, there," she called out in a resigned voice. "Can I help you?"

"I'm Rosalie Bennett. I have an interview with Sophia. Are you Sophia?"

"Yes," she said with forced cheerfulness. "However, there are days when I wish I weren't. And this is one of them," she mumbled quietly.

She moved to the sitting area, extending her arm and saying, "I'm sorry. Please come and take this chair here so we can talk."

"Who was doing all that yelling?"

"Oh, don't worry. His bark is much worse than his bite. You won't have to deal with him anyway."

I like to be in charge of an interview. I only know how to do that by asking the interviewer as many questions as they ask me. So I began. "How long have you been working for PUP?"

Sophia, a little startled by the question, smoothly answered. "Since its inception."

Now it was her turn. "What made you decide to apply to PUP?"

"I want to find a part-time position with some flexibility that leaves me some free time," I answered with a practiced smile. "This seems perfect!"

I felt that I was being watched, making me very uncomfortable. I pretended I had to get a Kleenex from my purse, which gave me time to gaze surreptitiously around as I fumbled for a tissue. I saw a painting on the wall that didn't look as though it belonged there. Without a second hesitation, I knew someone was watching me. I believed that Sophia knew it as well, for she didn't even jump when the same voice as before bellowed at her from the back, "I think she'll be perfect, Sophia. Ask her to consider the other position."

Sophia's face flushed, for she sensed that I had caught on that, indeed, someone was watching us. "Rosalie, there is another position that has opened up. I think you might be interested in it. It pays more money, and it has negotiable hours too. Are you interested in learning more about it?"

I envisioned myself at the Purple Passion Lounge's welcome desk directing people. "Oh, Gram, what am I getting myself into?" I grumbled silently, but she never appeared. I was on my own. "Sure. I'm always interested in seeing my choices, especially if they concern more money."

Pleased, Sophia smiled. "I think you'll like this offer. The person who was the main greeter at the Purple Passion Lounge had an untimely accident, and that position is now available."

At the look of distress on my face, Sophia explained, "Don't worry. You don't have to dance or do anything like that. All you have to do is look pretty. You've got that covered, my dear."

My concern was that I knew Sally's death wasn't an accident. I wanted to make Sophia and whoever else was listening believe that I rarely watched the news and didn't know much about her death. "I think I heard something about that, but don't follow the news that much. What happened?"

"Don't worry your pretty little head about it. Besides, nothing can be done about that now."

I didn't like Sophia making me sound like a dumb bimbo, so I stated more forcefully than I would typically use, "Well, I will have to have more information before making a decision. Exactly what will I have to do?"

"Act as the hostess welcoming clients to the lounge and assisting them with transportation when it's time to leave. By the way, that's where PUP comes in."

"Wouldn't I need to learn more about PUP before I can do that?"

Sophia gathered her thoughts like a light bulb was coming on. "Absolutely you do! That's why you would be working and training here with me for several days before starting your job at the Purple Passion Lounge. That way, at least, you could see if it will be a fit, right?"

I could easily hear the person in the back room clearing his throat in warning. Of what? I decided then and there to give this new job a try. "Well, Sophia, this sounds good, especially since I'll be working with you for a while. I don't like to start a job unless I know everything about it."

As I watched Sophia determinedly nod her head in agreement, I heard a throat being cleared even more loudly. Neither one of us looked his way. "No problem, Rosalie. That will give us plenty of time to prepare you for your new position. When are you available to begin?"

"How does tomorrow sound?" I answered gamely.

I left knowing there would be no turning back now. I amazed myself by forging ahead. I'm usually careful with my choices and can be exact about what I involve myself in. In addition, I almost always check out everything with my tarot cards before making a final decision. This time, I hadn't. Hmmm.

When I arrived home, Sweet Pea waited for me to greet her in the living room chair she claimed was hers. I don't know how we had gotten this welcoming part so mixed up. Isn't it the dog's role to greet her master? I guess not in my house. As soon as I suggested a walk, Sweet Pea looked up with a sweet expression, jumped down, and raced to the front door.

I was glad to walk with her and take the time to consider what I had just gotten myself into. No good was going to come of this, I knew. Yet my heart beat fast with the idea that perhaps I could be the one to find Melissa's killer. Strangely, it was something I now desperately wanted to do. Did this have to do with getting revenge for Jeff's death by beating the police at their own game and maybe exposing them for not always being the protectors of society they were expected to be?

I had to come to terms with how much I would use my psychic ability to help us search for Melissa's and Sally's killer or killers. After attending the School of Metaphysics, I learned how to expand and shut off information that seemed to flow to me. I could control the number of visions I allowed in and experienced. Also, I learned how to use my intuition and become better at balancing living my life and using my tarot cards or other spiritual modalities to validate my thoughts. What amazed me was that so many of us with expanded intuition can much more easily see things for others than ourselves. So, truth be told, I had come to rely on my grandmother more than I probably should; it might not have been the best thing to do.

Despite this, I perched on a small stone wall lining the sidewalk and called, "Hi, Gram, I need to check in with you. Are you available?"

There was a breeze rustling around me. Sweet Pea stopped and looked up at me expectantly. She seemed to know what was happening and lay down at my feet to wait. She had become used to Gram's visits. "Anything for you, Rosie girl!"

"Gram, I can't believe what I have done! There's time for me to back out if you think it'd be best. What do you think I should do?"

"My dear, sweet Rosie. You know this has to be your decision. I can't interfere with your journey and your choices. I will say this, however—you are in for quite a ride!"

"Oh, Gram. I know you're right, but I was just hoping …."

"Follow your heart. Love you." Her words trailed behind her as she went off. Knowing our conversation was over, Sweet Pea rose from her spot, wanting to continue our walk.

"Sometimes, Sweet Pea, I sure do wish you could talk," I said, patting her head and looking deep into her eyes.

I had to laugh because I could swear by the expression on her little face that I wouldn't always like what she had to say if she could talk.

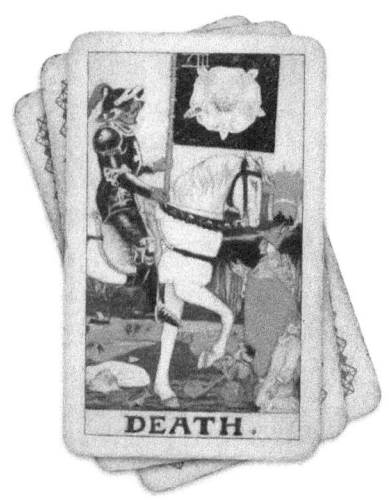

CHAPTER 14

T he next morning, not knowing how I was expected to dress, I carefully chose leggings and a top between casual and more tailored business casual wear. I gathered my dark, flowing tresses into a ponytail to control them and headed out to meet Sophia at the PUP office.

I didn't know what to expect regarding what we would cover in training, but I was curious to find out. Sophia was waiting for me with a smile. I didn't hear anyone else in the office; there was no shouting or throat-clearing. As she noticed me looking around, Sophia spoke. "Nobody here but us chickens."

I laughed at the old joke and said, "Good."

"Before we get started, it goes without saying that our training is confidential. I feel confident from our interview yesterday that I can trust you to adhere to that. So, for now, we'll start with the procedures for PUP and see what comes after that. Ready?" she asked.

"Sure," I answered, aware that this first day was a test.

"Since you applied for the position of PUP driver, you already know some of the rules. Once you apply and are accepted as a driver, your car is inspected to be sure it's in proper shape. No junkers—only well-maintained and late-model cars. Also, we install a tracker to locate the drivers during off-hours when they're unavailable to drive." She paused, looking at me intently before adding, "Not every driver knows this. If necessary, we can override any turned-off tracker to find out exactly where they are."

"Oh," I said, playing dumb while my brain went wild with this new information, thinking this is what must have happened with Melissa. "Is this something you tell your drivers?"

"Not necessarily. That's something I decide after their interview with me."

That, I thought, meant after the loud noise from the back office had a chance to spy on the applicant. So much for honesty on her part.

"In your position at the Purple Passion, you'll be notified by one of the girls when a party is getting ready to leave. They are trained to check with their client to see if he needs transportation, which is where PUP comes in. Instead of calling a cab company, you'll have a list of certain PUP telephone numbers to call. The girls will advise you which number to call. These special PUP drivers know the routine and make themselves available to take on departing client or clients."

"You mean, I never know who the person is I'm calling?"

"It's better that way. Besides, there's really no need to know because our security guards are the ones who lead the clients and load them into the PUP car."

Sophia gave a small, embarrassed chuckle and said, "I should say, guide them into the PUP car, shouldn't I?"

I knew what she meant. The Purple Passion Lounge got their clients drunk enough that "loading" them, most likely with an empty wallet, into the car certainly was the correct wording. "What's next?" I asked.

We spent the rest of the day reviewing the procedures for interviewing potential drivers, the paperwork needed, and other things. After I filled out my paperwork for payroll, Sophia smiled and said, "You did very well, Rosie. You can leave now. I'll see you tomorrow."

I looked confused, as I had been there a mere four hours, so she added, "Don't worry, Rosie, you'll be paid for the full day. Everything is okay. We're getting along just fine."

I left PUP's office feeling exhilarated and more than a little pumped by what I had learned. I could feel my heart pounding with excitement as I realized we might be able to nail Melissa's and Sally's killer(s) between Brian and me. At the moment, I couldn't think of anything that would please me more.

I had a pretty good idea of what was happening at PUP and needed to talk to Brian about it. My thinking of him prompted him to telephone me as I headed home.

"Hey, Rosie, how's it going?"

"Very fascinating here on my end. How about you?"

"Some interesting stuff with me too. Let's get together. How about meeting at Sam's Roadhouse at 5 o'clock, and we can go over it then?"

"Sounds good to me. Just don't be late!" I warned, hating to sit alone in a bar.

"Never for you." He added smoothly.

Nothing seemed to rattle him, I thought. He was so unlike Jeff. Yet, they both pulled at me in much the same way. What was it about them? Jeff had seen the world almost as if it were a book of rules to be followed. Brian seemed aware of those same rules but played them out differently. I had trusted Jeff implicitly and was devastated to live through all the accusations others had made about him after his untimely death. I knew psychically those damaging accusations had been false. Still, things had happened so quickly with his cremation and closing the door on further possibilities that I never had the chance or the courage to pursue them. Again, I was convinced the Chief of Police was at the bottom of it. Boy, did I ever want to prove it!

When I returned home, I greeted Sweet Pea and gave her a treat simply because I wanted to, which caused her to prance at my feet in appreciation. I headed for the office to make notes about my first day at PUP so I wouldn't forget anything.

Afterward, I checked my emails and noticed an odd one. It was entitled BEWARE and made my heart jump. I opened it to find "Be careful. You are heading into territory that's dangerous for you. You know what happens then. ☹"

I clicked on the sender's address at the top of the email —mail-noreply@gmail.com—which was scary because there was no such person or any way to trace it back to the sender. I felt sick to my stomach because I knew exactly what happens. All I had to do was remember Melissa and Sally. I decided to print out the email to show it to Brian.

96

Why was I so determined to proceed with investigating their deaths? Was it because I sat back and had done nothing to dispel the accusations about Jeff after his death?

I got out my tarot cards and shuffled them. It was time to pick my card for the day, and I was curious to see what would turn up. I remixed the cards. Then I quickly pulled one from the deck—the High Priestess! The card's meaning was not what I wanted—"Other people's advice won't help here. Stick to your own opinion." Hmmm. I was on my own then.

As I put this card back in the deck, the Death card poked its head halfway out. It seemed stuck until I gently pushed it back with the other cards. That's interesting, I thought. A warning, perhaps? I'd have to be cautious about what was going on around me. I let out a long sigh. I knew I wasn't responsible for any death if the Death card popped up from my tarot cards. Yet, why was it warning me that one might occur?

It was time to feed Sweet Pea and change my clothes before I met Brian. I was glad we were meeting, especially in light of the unsolicited email. It frightened me.

I'm amazed by how much new technology takes all privacy from everyone. We all have seen the privacy notices that theoretically are there to protect us but don't. It's even scarier to know that whatever you research online can be seen and filed in categories. Then you continually get ads about the subjects you were studying popping up on your computer screen. It's disturbing to know those who can break into a supposedly secure system can extract private information and sell it to those who have the potential to hurt us. That has happened on a large scale in our country several times, and I'm sure there will be more times to come.

I scolded myself. "Just deal with it!" I was now in a fitful state and hurried to Sam's Roadhouse.

I arrived at five o'clock sharp and was relieved to find Brian's car in the parking lot. As I entered, I shouted a little too eagerly from the doorway, "Hi, Cowboy!"

He looked up and seemed surprised to see me so enthused about seeing him. "What's up, Sunshine? Come have a seat," he added cheerfully as he pulled out a chair for me.

He noticed I was a bit out of breath. He studied the worry lines crossing my brow and asked with concern, "What's the matter?"

Before I sat down, I rooted through my purse and pulled out the printed email. "Here, read this and tell me what you think."

As he read it, I noticed Brian frown. He looked up from the paper to ask, "Where did this come from? Was this sent to your private email?"

I nodded yes and held my breath to hear what he would say next.

"I don't like this at all! Did you check to see where it originated?"

"Yes, mail-noreply@gmail.com."

"You know there is no such thing, right? It's called phishing."

"Yes, I know that, but what does it mean?" I sighed, recalling my earlier thoughts regarding the internet.

"Okay, calm down. Let's look at this logically," he said, sounding much like Jeff had been in his policeman mode.

"I think that most people wouldn't know that you are looking into the deaths of Melissa and Sally, right? So it must have something to do with your taking on a position at PUP or the Purple Passion Lounge, correct?"

He looked at me, waiting for me to agree. Instead, I envisioned a few people gathered around a casket saying, "What a shame. She was so young." I was trying to see who was in the coffin but was blocked from doing so by the same large, rough man I saw in my vision at the time of Sally's death.

"Hey, Rosie! Did you hear what I said?" he asked as he shook my arm gently.

"I'm sorry. What?"

"I think it must have something to do with your job at PUP or the Purple Passion Lounge. Don't you agree?"

Intuitively, I knew Brian was right. Someone did not want me there, but why? What did they not want me to find out? The stress of what this email meant was beginning to give me a headache. I turned to Brian. "Yes, I agree. We'll find out soon enough what's going on, won't we?"

"Listen, believe me, you don't have to be involved in any of this. It's okay with me if you want to bail. I think you should. We just have to figure out how to keep you safe."

There was no way I was willing to back out now. I felt more alive than I had in a very long time. I wanted to know more than ever why two young women, girls really, had been killed, and their deaths seemed unimportant to the police. "No, Brian, you can count me in. I want to get to the bottom of it all."

"Are you sure?"

"Positively sure." I quickly changed the conversation, "Now, please, it's time for a nice glass of wine. Let's relax. I want to hear all about what's happening in your world."

Sitting there, I couldn't get my latest vision out of my thoughts. I tried pushing it away. I rested my head on my hands to mentally relax while I waited for Brian to return with our drinks. I was curious to hear what he had to say.

Brian placed our glasses of wine on the table. We each took a sip, not bothering to toast each other. Instead of telling me how his day had unfolded, he wanted to know more about my two sessions at PUP. He was not himself. He was in a very different frame of mind, reminding me again of Jeff in his policeman mode. He was all business. His questions were direct, and he demanded details of each part of my conversations with Sophia.

I could see the waitress heading our way. As she reached our table, Brian turned and snapped, "Not now. I will let you know if we need anything."

The waitress was surprised. The last time we had been here, he had been very friendly, even jolly. At first, I thought she believed he might have been joking. Brian continued to stare at her and didn't utter another word. She hightailed it back to the bar area, obviously a bit distressed.

I asked, "Was that necessary?"

"Yes. We've got a lot to cover here. We need to devise a plan to make sure you are safe. We don't have time to waste."

"Just what do you have in mind?" I asked sarcastically. "I want you to go through everything that happened at PUP today. Don't leave out a thing."

After filling Brian in on all that had been said and done, I turned to him. "Well, what now?"

He thought for a moment and said, "We both have iPhones, and we both know how to record on them, right? We have to make sure to keep our phones in silent mode. Do you keep your phone with you at all times?"

"Unfortunately—and I guess now it's fortunate—I do."

"Any time you're involved in a meeting, set up your phone to record if possible. Understand? Then let's look at putting a special tracker on your car, so I can see where you are, okay?"

"How are you going to do that? Don't you need special equipment?"

"No worries. I have a friend who'll take care of everything. I will ask you again—are you sure you want to continue helping me with this investigation?"

"Absolutely. I believe the Chief of Police is involved somehow, and if I can nail him …."

"Wait! Why do you think that, Rosie?"

"It's a long story," I said, not wanting to wade through it all.

"Does this have something to do with your fiancé?" he asked intently.

"How do you know about that?" I asked in astonishment.

"Remember, I'm a newsman. I had a chance to read up on it when I was doing some research on the Chief of Police. I, too, believe he's involved in some way."

"Oh," I said, relieved to know we were on the same side. "What else did you find out about our wonderful Chief of Police?"

"Quite a bit, actually. First, the chief claims he graduated from Boston University but completed only two years there. He did so poorly that he was forced to join the Marines to avoid more trouble with the police for drunken and disorderly conduct. He claims that becoming a Marine saved his life. However, digging further into it, I discovered he was discharged early without reason. Something is up with that."

"Who are his connections here then, I wonder?"

"I don't know, other than the obvious. I'm going to be watching him closely for the next few days. He has become very defensive about the police department in general. He seems to ignore the press asking questions about the murders. Something else is going on."

"What about your boss at Channel 5 News?"

"Whenever I mention anything about the murders, he waves his hand at me and tells me to leave his office. He says to find something better to report about. Very strange, don't you think?"

"More like he's taking orders from someone else," I added reflectively.

"I think so too. That's why I will tail the Chief of Police for a while and see who his friends are."

"Have you been back to the Purple Passion Lounge?" I asked innocently.

Brian blushed and said in a firm voice, "I need to talk to Tony, and he's been successful at ignoring me as a newsman. I should become a regular client. I'll drop in for a drink or two at night. That way, when you're working there, I'll already have established myself as a regular. Good idea, don't you think?"

I chuckled to myself, knowing he just wanted my approval of what he was doing. It certainly wasn't up to me to approve or disapprove. Frankly, I thought there'd be value in having him there when I worked, so I nodded, answering, "Sure."

"By the way, when will you start working at the lounge?"

"In a few more days. Probably Monday."

I stared at him until he looked at his watch and said, "Well, I guess I had better get going. Let's stay in touch. I'll call you tomorrow, or you call me, okay?"

"Sounds like a plan, Stan," I replied with a smile.

"Let me walk you to your car, then."

Brian took out his wallet and pulled some bills from it. Although we had only two glasses of wine, he was looking for our waitress to hand her an extra tip and an apology. I watched as Brian discreetly looked around, searching the faces of the customers filing into the bar. I felt the hair on the back of my neck rise, and I looked back at the corner where we had been sitting. A rather large man had taken our spot, and I could see only the back of his head, but something about him bothered me; I wasn't sure what.

They say ignorance is bliss, and now that I was aware that I could be in danger, I saw threats everywhere.

J.S. Peck

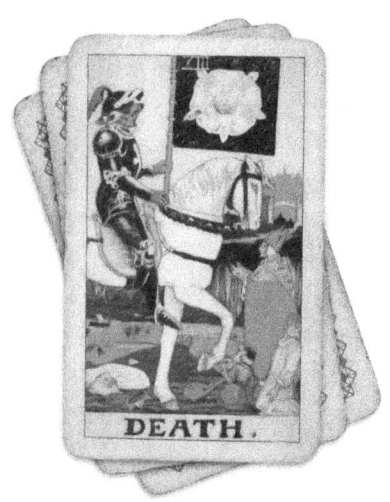

CHAPTER 15

S ophia was in a good mood the following day and greeted me warmly. I hadn't slept well but responded cheerfully, "Good morning, Boss!"

She was surprised by being called Boss. She chuckled, adding, "That'll be the day."

I followed her to the two desks we'd worked at the day before. She handed me a file folder with information about one of the PUP drivers. A second folder was lying next to where the first file had been. "I want you to go through both folders and let me know if you see a difference between the two."

I hesitated, then looked at her and said, "Okay."

I flipped open the first driver's folder and studied it briefly. There was one I-9 form for verification and a W-4 form for payroll information. In addition, there was a company form where the driver had filled in the requested information on make, model, year of car he would be driving, and cell phone number. There was also a number I couldn't identify written across the top of the form. No application, resume, letters of reference, background check information, or drug test verification existed. In addition, there was no proof his car insurance was current. After scanning the file, I looked up at Sophia in surprise. "Oh my, Sophia, is this all there is?"

"Just look through the other file and see if there are any differences," she prodded.

I laid down the first file and reached for the second. As I did so, I heard the office's back door open and slam closed, followed by heavy footsteps.

"Oh, dear. Just hide the files and pretend you are doing something else. Quick!" Sophia added hurriedly.

"Good morning, sir. I didn't expect you in today. Is everything okay?" Sophia called out as she rose from her chair and headed to the back office.

I couldn't hear anything but mumbled sounds, which rose in pitch. After a few minutes, I heard heavy steps retreating to the back door, then silence. Sophia returned a short while later, looking a bit frazzled.

"Are you okay?" I asked.

"Yes, and no. I'm in a predicament."

Worry creased her brow. She appeared to be weighing a decision. Finally, she asked in a low voice, "I need to be able to trust you. Can I?"

"Of course, you can," I replied earnestly.

"I don't want a glib response, Rosie. Let me ask you again. Can I trust you completely?"

"Yes, Sophia, you can. Cross my heart," I replied, meaning it as I looked her straight in the eye.

"All right, dear. I believe you. There is something about you that makes me believe that I can trust you. That's why I thought training you in what is going on at PUP was a good idea. Let me explain a few things. I don't know where else to turn."

"Sophia, you can count on me, honest."

"You remind me so much of me at your age, when I was enthusiastic about life and believed the best of everyone."

She shook her head in dismay as she sat back in her chair, recalling her memories. "I was just 18 when I first came to Las Vegas. I was so naïve about everything! I thought then I was beautiful enough to get whatever I wanted. For me, that was to be a big star on stage as a singer. Well, things didn't go very well, as you can imagine. Suddenly, I found myself pregnant and without a job. The only way left for me to bring in some money was to become a dancer in one of the older men's lounges.

"It is there I met a man I thought wonderful then. I married him just in time, so the baby appeared to be his. He and I both knew better, though. It didn't seem to bother him initially, but as a few years passed, it became an issue. Anyone could plainly see our son didn't look like either of us, and his friends constantly kidded my husband about it, especially since we had no other children. One night, my husband lost control and smacked our son so hard that it threw him across the room. I called the cops on him. My husband never forgave me. We were quietly divorced shortly after that incident. I haven't seen him since."

She hesitated. "Do you want me to continue?"

I couldn't figure out where this conversation was going, but I was curious. "Of course, Sophia. Go ahead."

"Good," she responded with noticeable relief. "It was my boss who saved me. I began working for the company where I am now. There were only two of us initially, the man you heard in the office earlier and me. Originally, he was a talent scout and agent looking for headliners for the Las Vegas Strip. Back then, he had so many beautiful young girls who needed money for one reason or another come to him for help that it was difficult for him to ignore them. He soon realized he could solve his and their financial problems by opening up an upscale lounge for men. The girls acted as hostesses, always remaining dressed and available to sit with the men while they drank or ate their meals. Afterward, if the men requested it, they could dance formally with them to the sound of big-band music or softer music. It was a kind of old-fashioned club. Remember, in those days, all the women wore gowns, and the men wore suits or tuxes."

She became lost in her story until I urged, "Go on, Sophia; please continue."

"Making ends meet became harder and harder when our competition went to sexier means to satisfy the male clientele. My boss even gave me a small percentage of the business to keep me on. It meant the world to me to be acknowledged that way because we both knew he could never have kept the business running without me. Then, we reached the point in our business when we had a choice. Although I was not happy about the small changes we made to make our lounge appear sexier, I went along with them. I thought we could keep everything under control and decent and make money. And we did ... for a while."

Sophia looked around nervously, almost as though expecting someone to listen in. "We continued to have some financial troubles because of increasing competition. Instead of closing the business while we were still ahead, my boss allowed a silent partner to join us. Oddly, I was never told or allowed to know who it was. That was part of the agreement. It still makes me mad to think of it! Now I'm so involved in all that's going on that there isn't much I can do to straighten things out. Just so you know, in everything to do with him, we reference him as 'B. B.'"

My heart thumped so loud I thought Sophia must be able to hear it. I forced myself to remain calm and not reveal that the reference meant something. "Isn't that strange?" I asked in a soft voice.

Sophia continued. "I'm determined to find out who that is. I don't like being a part of the business at the Purple Passion with their drug issues and prostitution. It has become completely unprofessional and cheesy. Now we have PUP involved as part of it all," she added with a disgruntled puff.

"Hmm … so what are you going to do?"

"I'll tell you what I'm going to do. I'll find out who this B. B. is and give him more than a piece of my mind."

I watched a grin spread across Sophia's face, and she laughed at herself for sounding so old-fashioned. "I sound so stupid, I know."

"Do you think any girl who works at the Purple Passion Lounge is in danger?" I asked, feeling cautious about what I'd just learned. I thought of the two young girls who had been involved with the lounge and were dead.

"Oh, no, not at all. Only the girls who do more than dance seem to get into trouble. They aren't always ethical, and the temptation of more money can sometimes get in the way. And Rosie, if I thought you'd be in danger in that position, I would rip up your employment contract right now! So no, my dear, in your hostess position, I think you're completely safe."

I wasn't feeling so safe. With worry beginning to eat me, I asked, "So how do I fit into all of this, Sophia?"

"I don't want you involved in anything but keeping your ears and eyes open for who our silent partner might be, understand? Nothing else."

"Yes, I understand." I was beginning to get excited about being the hostess at the Purple Passion Lounge. It would allow me to scout around the lounge without being obvious. I would love to take down B. B. if he were the cause of Melissa and Sally's murders! I was eager, and my heart pounded at that thought. I liked this aspect of my detective work already.

"Well, I suppose we'd better get back to the files," stated Sophia

"Sounds good to me," I responded, eager to see the difference between the two.

As I went through the second file, it seemed only slightly thicker, with just two extra sheets above and beyond what had been in the first file—an application and a copy of the driver's auto insurance. Still no resume, letter of reference, background check, or drug test verification. "Sophia?" I called out.

"Yes, Rosie."

"I understand that all the PUP drivers are independent contractors. Is that right?"

"Yes, they are."

"Does that mean they don't need to complete the other documents?"

"Although we have them complete an application for the information, we don't put it in their file. If we need to hand over the files to any authority, we don't want to confuse them or have them think any driver is an employee, so we keep them separate in the file cabinet. Remind me to show you that later."

"Hmm. I guess that makes sense. Other than the application and insurance form in the second file, they seem alike. That is, except for two things."

"Yes?" asked Sophia.

"Number one, the first file doesn't have the driver's insurance form, and number two, there's a different number written at the top of the automobile form. What's that for?"

"Ah," she said. "Good. I'm glad you asked me. That's the number that lets us override their tracking device."

"How come not all of them have one?"

"Well, that's exactly what I wanted to know when I noticed the first one. When I asked my boss about it, he said, "Sophia, we have known each other for years. As much as I don't agree with everything that's happening, there are a few things I won't discuss with you. This is one of them."

After I got all huffy and puffy with him, he turned to me and said in a soft voice, "I don't want you to get hurt. The more you don't know, the better off you are."

My mind raced with thoughts, not all pleasant. Something was not right. "Sophia, are you sure that you should be poking around? Remember, 'curiosity killed the cat.'"

She turned to me, forcefully reminding me, "But 'satisfaction brought him back.' No, Rosie, I have had enough. I have to get to the bottom of this."

We looked through a number of the other files. I began to type into the computer names of some drivers with override numbers written across their auto information page. We laughingly named it "mincemeat pie" since that is what we hoped B. B. would be after we caught him. We then put that document into a desktop folder we labeled "Recipes," believing that no one other than us would be interested in opening the folder.

I downloaded some actual recipes from the internet and added them to the recipe folder to make them look more authentic. Sophia called out, "I'll finish up. You've had enough, so call it a day. I'll see you tomorrow."

I felt mentally and emotionally exhausted. I was more than glad to head home. What would tomorrow bring? For some reason, I thought it wasn't going to be good.

CHAPTER 16

B rian called me on my car phone when I was on the way home. "How was your day?"

"Interesting. How was yours?"

"Not much going on, to be honest. Everyone seems willing to let things slip, as though nothing like the death of two women—two prostitutes, they've now called them—just happened. Simply old news and not a priority. I thought I would head to the Purple Passion Lounge this evening for 'investigative' reasons."

I smiled and chose not to tease him about his choice of words. "Okay, let's meet tomorrow to review where we are. Sound good?"

"If I can make it after a long night of spending time with all that sexiness," he teased.

Immediately irritated, I said, "Oh, for God's sake, Cowboy!"

"Oh, my, testy, are we?"

"Just tired," I sighed, annoyed by my foolish reaction.

"Okay, I'll call you tomorrow, or better yet, why don't we meet at Sam's at 5?

"I'll be there. Have fun tonight," I said and quickly hung up so I wouldn't hear what Brian had to say about my being cranky.

After putting my notes of the day into my computer, I took Sweet Pea for a quick walk before dinner. Afterward, we snuggled in for a movie on Netflix. To my surprise, I immediately fell asleep and woke up after the film had ended, finding a message across my television screen asking if I were still there.

I dragged myself to bed and collapsed onto it without even brushing my teeth. Sweet Pea looked at me in surprise. She was used to my nightly rituals and knew something was off. I cuddled her next to me and closed my eyes again, off to a dreamland that was anything but peaceful.

I kept dreaming of all types of cats, even the cartoon cat Felix, always with the words curiosity and satisfaction swirling around in all kinds of unpleasant ways. Once again, I dreamed of the funeral scene where I couldn't see who was in the casket. I tossed and turned until I woke up around 4 a.m. I couldn't get back to sleep, so after 30 minutes or so, I finally got out of bed. Before heading downstairs for a cup of coffee, I looked at Sweet Pea peacefully on the top of the bed with one eye open, watching me. She was there to stay and not about to get up this early.

"I don't blame you," I mumbled, leaving the room.

My stomach was a bit upset, and the coffee tasted bitter. I put it down and went to get the tarot cards. "Gram," I called out. "I don't know what's going on with me. Am I being stupid to get even more involved in all this?"

I felt the air move around me and smelled her scent as I heard her response. "Rosie girl, there comes a time when we step out of our comfort zone to be or do something very different from what we know or are comfortable with. That is what life is all about."

"I know," I responded, sounding like the little girl I had been long ago.

Just as she had done when I was little, she said the same thing she used to say—"Maybe you should listen to your heart. You'll know what to do then."

"Thanks, Gram. You're no help at all … but I still love you," I said with a smile.

"Love you too, Sunshine." Off she went into the atmosphere, her unique scent trailing behind her.

I sighed, got out my tarot cards, and shuffled them. I closed my eyes and asked the cards out loud, "Is it in my highest good to stay involved with PUP and the Purple Passion Lounge?"

As I drew one card out, there was another stuck to it. I pulled them apart, face down. Slowly, I picked up the first one to find the Two of Swords. Its meaning wouldn't give me a clear answer, for it was "Don't put up a smoke screen. Dare to explore, look inside yourself, and go beyond the obvious, indecision." Yet, it was a number two card, meaning partnerships.

I decided not to look at the other card. I quickly shoved it back into the deck but caught a glimpse at what might have been the Death card. Maybe nothing would happen if I didn't pay any attention to it. Shaking off how ridiculous that seemed, I was determined to proceed with the investigation, with or without the Death card. After all, "in for a penny, in for a pound."

The doorbell rang. I glanced at the clock, wondering who could be at the door early at 6 a.m. I peeked through the peephole as Sweet Pea bounced down the stairs and stood barking at my feet, her tail wagging in anticipation. Sure enough, the only fool up and out this early was Brian. I opened the door and could smell him before he stepped inside. "Whew! You smell like booze and cigarettes!"

"I know. I just left the Purple Passion. What a night!"

"Please. The only details I'm interested in are those that have anything to do with our investigation."

"Party pooper," he teased. "How about some coffee?"

As I watched Brian maneuver toward the kitchen, a thought came to me. He looked and acted drunk, but somehow I knew he wasn't. Was it all an act?

"Cowboy?"

"Yes, Sunshine?" There it was again. My grandmother called me Sunshine a few minutes ago, and here he was with the same nickname. Odd.

"You can stop playacting now," I said to test him.

Brian immediately stood up straight and laughingly asked, "Did I fool you?"

"I have to admit that you're pretty good."

"Well, let's hope the people at the Purple Passion Lounge think so too. I'm beginning to understand how they work it there, and it's a bit scary. Certainly profitable for them, though."

"Here's some coffee. Tell me what you found out, and I'll see whether it matches what I know."

Brian looked excited as he said, "Well, I'm certainly beginning to learn more about Tony Angelo, who owns and manages the Purple Passion Lounge. All the girls are hush-hush about what goes on there. They're afraid to cross Tony and end up like Melissa and Sally. But one girl said she thought Sally was Tony's cousin or another family member. She overheard him on the phone yelling at his mother, defending himself about Sally's death. As soon as another girl came by, she immediately shifted onto my lap and … well, you know," he added with pink cheeks. "Oh, sorry, Rosie," he said, looking not at all apologetic.

I ignored him while trying to figure out how the man I saw pushing through the crowd at Sally's death fit into all of this. I came up with nothing.

"By the way, I saw David Masterly, the guy in charge of the girls. He looks like death warmed over. The girls say he's lost a lot of weight and has not been himself since Melissa's death. He can't even speak her name without tears filling his eyes. The shock of Sally's death while he was in Hawaii, added to Melissa's, has him ignoring all the girls, they say."

"Wow, that's too bad. Maybe his relationship with Melissa was more than her being one of the girls. What do you think?"

"Certainly worth looking into again. Oh, and David's wife dropped in to see him while I was there. Let me tell you, she is a piece of work. Even the hairs on my neck stood up when I saw her. I don't envy him dealing with the likes of her."

"Oh, my, really as bad as all that?"

"For sure. What did you learn at PUP yesterday, Rosie?"

"Guess who the silent partner of the Purple Passion Lounge is?"

He threw out his hands. "I give up. Who?"

"You mean you're not even going to guess? That's no fun."

"Howdy, Doody?"

"Ha ha! Try B. B."

"You mean the same guy who gave a diamond ring to Melissa?" he asked as his cheeks grew pinker.

I noticed his sensitivity to B.B. and his glowing cheeks. I ignored them and answered, "The same."

"No clues as to who it is?"

"Nope. Even Sophia doesn't know. In the books, anything to do with him is always referenced as B. B. By the way, did you know Sophia is part owner of the Purple Passion Lounge as well? She was furious when they kept upping the sexiness there, and now she's even more upset with all that's happening there. She's vowed to find out who B. B. is and set things right."

"Hold on. Sophia better be careful. What she's doing could get her hurt. And you—*you* could be in big trouble too."

I remained silent, lost in the truth of what he'd said.

"How much longer are you working with Sophia there at PUP?"

"Just one more day. After that, I begin training as one of the hostesses at the lounge. But not until Monday."

"Right," Brian responded, looking a bit uncomfortable. "Well, here's my plan. I'll continue looking into the ownership of the Purple Passion Lounge and see what I can find out. I'll also check out the ownership of PUP. I should've done that before anyway," he added, disgusted with himself. "My boss has been keeping me busy on all sorts of stories regarding anything unrelated to the deaths of Melissa and Sally. That's why I've let things get behind."

"I'll see what I can do on my end. I'll pump Sophia for more information."

"See if you can record anything. That's the most important thing you can do right now."

"That's not easy face-to-face, but I'll do what I can."

"Okay then."

He checked his watch and jumped up. "I'd better be off. See you later at Sam's?"

"I'll have to let you know, okay?"

I looked at the clock and realized I had better get going too. I sighed. Another day, another dollar.

CHAPTER 17

I was late for work. A car accident had cars trapped for miles on the highway. I knew better than to take this route, I fumed. I promised myself from now on, I would always take the back roads. When I arrived at PUP, I was in a snit and ready to bark at anyone who looked at me wrong. Intuitively, I knew to set my phone on record and vibrate before I went in.

"Hey, girl. What happened to you?" asked Sophia when I got inside. As soon as she saw the look on my face, she added, "No worries. Come in, fix yourself a cup of coffee, and unwind. "Were you caught in that mess on the highway?"

I nodded, grateful she wasn't upset. "Sure was. What a mess, with cars all over the place. I'm just glad I got here in one piece."

"So am I," she added. "We have a full day ahead right here. We'll start training at the lounge on Monday; sound good?"

"Yes. I'm looking forward to that, so that you know." Sophia smiled and nodded her head. "Good."

I was curious about what she was going to show me next. After I sipped my coffee and settled myself, Sophia called me to her desk. "Rosie, pull up a chair and join me."

As she pulled out a journal and laid it flat on her desk, she asked me again, "I can trust you, right?"

I nodded, saying, "Yes, for sure," despite feeling dread.

"Okay then. What I am about to show you is strictly confidential, something to keep to yourself, or I could get in trouble. I'm showing this to you because there's been a leak of some of this information, and it's not me. The bosses are trying to find out how she got the information in the first place and what she's done with it. I also want to see whether the code is too easy, something she could've figured out."

"Why don't you just ask the girl who took it?"

"Not possible. That's why I trust you."

My heart skipped a beat. I could feel my face flushing. My God, I knew who she was talking about—Melissa!

"Are you okay?" Sophia asked as she searched my face.

"Yes, I'm having a hot flash from the coffee. It's a bit strong for me—I normally have decaf." I quickly changed the subject. "Who else did you say has access to this information?"

"Just the three of us—my boss, B. B., and now me—no one else."

"Where is this information kept?"

"In the safe. You're looking at a special set of books for information only. So that you know, we also keep a second set of financials for the IRS and tax purposes. Okay, let's take a look here. The figures are figures, but can you make out anything else?"

"Well, I can see some repeats, which I assume are clients' names?"

"That's right. What else?"

"In addition, it appears there can be a different name connected with that same client name, right?"

"Yes, that's right. Can you decipher anything else?"

I studied the information and saw it was filled with anagrams and numbers. Yes, it would take me a while, but I believed I could get this right if given enough time. Instead, I hesitated and lied, saying, "Gosh! I'm not sure I'll be able to, Sophia! It's so complicated. Maybe if you give me some more time."

"Hmmph. I think I know exactly what is going on," she said in a harsh voice, looking at me intently. My heart began to race, making me wonder whether she had guessed I had lied.

"This has something to do with B. B., I know it. Just take a bit more time, Rosie, and then we'll move on to something else. Wait, don't even bother! It doesn't matter, for I know it all ends with B. B."

My heart lurched as I felt the phone in my pants pocket vibrate. My phone had been recording since I had programmed it before entering the office. I didn't want to draw any attention to my having a phone with me, especially since we had been discussing confidential material. I needed to walk away. I rose abruptly, saying, "Damn! I can't wait any longer! Sorry, but I need to use the bathroom now."

As I headed toward it, I grabbed my purse and called back to her, "Too much coffee."

Sophia just stood there with a funny expression on her face. She might have heard my phone vibrate despite the message alert sound on low. Since the sound didn't last long, perhaps I had gotten away without Sophia's hearing it. Once in the bathroom, I looked at the phone, which showed a message from Brian, "Give me a call on your way home. Can't meet you tonight."

"Now what?" I wondered. I felt let down by the thought of not seeing Brian and sharing information. Oh, well. I hurriedly flushed the toilet, dropped my phone into my purse, and rushed out of the bathroom to meet Sophia.

"Okay, Boss, I'm ready to go!" I called out to an empty room.

"Over here, Rosie." Sophia was speaking with an older gentleman. He wore typical work clothes with "PUP" on his shirt pocket. He talked to her softly and waved his finger in front of her.

I could barely make out his words, "I don't like this one bit."

"Not now, Sam. We'll talk later."

As I approached them, he looked at me with a flicker in his eyes as if he recognized me. He smiled and said in a slight Irish brogue, "Hello there!"

I extended my hand and looked intently at him. "Do I know you?"

"You probably don't remember me, but I would know you anywhere with that mop of hair," he said with a laugh and a twinkle in his eyes.

Noting my expression, he laughed again. "I used to know your grandmother years ago. I remember you from when you were just a wee little thing. You have the same hair and look like her too. She was a great lady," he added with a smile.

"Oh," I said.

He gave me a friendly pat on the shoulder and turned away. "Well, I must be pushing off, Sophia. I have another car to do. Don't worry, take it easy; we'll talk later."

Sophia nodded her head and gave a long sigh. She seemed to be lost in thought until I gave a slight cough. She turned my way. "That sure is a good man."

"I noticed he's wearing a PUP uniform. What does he do?"

He inspects the cars of those who want to become PUP drivers. He's the one who installs the trackers in them for those chosen few."

"He seemed a bit upset. Is everything okay?"

"Not really," she answered mysteriously.

"Does he inspect the cars of everyone who fills out the application?"

"No, not necessarily—just those my boss and I have approved. Not everyone who applies is allowed to drive for us."

"How come?"

"Well, they are chosen only if they are willing to drive for the Purple Passion Lounge. And truthfully, we want only a limited number of those drivers."

Things were beginning to make sense. PUP was a shell company quickly established and doing just enough business to look legitimate. So what was the real deal?

We continued listing the drivers with trackers on their cars, placing them in the Recipes icon on the computer. Sophia looked at her watch and said, "I'm so sorry, Rosie, but I have a splitting headache. I don't feel well. I'm going to lie down for a bit. Do you think you could finish up here by yourself?"

When I looked up, Sophia stood with her shoulders slumped and her face a pasty white. "Are you sure you're okay?" I asked.

"Don't worry. A short nap will fix me up just fine."

"Okay, I sure hope you feel better. Let me know if you need anything. I'll knock on your office door in a little while to make sure you're all right."

"That'll be fine, Rosie. Thank you."

As I watched her make her way to her office, I sensed something was vitally wrong. She was walking in a crooked line, somewhat out of balance. I called out, "Are you sure you're okay?"

"Yes, just a spot of vertigo, I think."

"Just let me know if I can do anything."

She waved her hand at me and continued. I returned to finish the list we'd been working on, filling in as much detail as possible. Hours later, I thought to take advantage of this time alone to use the thumb drive I had in my purse to download the list onto it. I grabbed my purse, pulled out the thumb drive, and inserted it into the computer to download. As I did, I heard the back door slam open, and Sophia's boss yelled, "Damn it, Sophia, where are you?"

I could hear Sam behind him, "Now, calm down. She'd do nothing to hurt you, and you know that."

"Sophia?" her boss hollered again. He slammed open another door, presumably Sophia's office door. Then came complete silence for what must have been close to a minute before the two men began wailing.

As they both cried out Sophia's name, I began to tremble. I intuitively knew what must have happened. I crept to the doorway. Sophia was lying on the couch in her office, unmoving and appearing sound asleep. It was the color of her lips that gave it away. They were blue and set in a grimace. It was that noise that made the two men turn my way. Sophia's boss was the man I had seen in my vision at the time of Sally's murder. He was staring at me now with anger. "How could you have let this happen? Why didn't you call for help?"

Tears filled my eyes, and I began to weep. I stood still, paralyzed by his accusations.

Before I could even respond, Sam came to my defense. "Don't go there. You can easily see she must've had a heart attack. Nobody can help that."

I blurted out, "Sophia said she had a headache and wanted to rest. Take just a short nap, she said."

Her boss looked at me, eyes tragic and filled with tears that spilled over. "Sam, get her the hell out of here!"

As I turned to flee from them, he added, "And stay with her and make sure you lock the door after her. Don't let anyone in! No one can find her body here after all the bad publicity we've gotten between PUP and the Purple Passion Lounge. They would conclude that her death was another murder instead of a heart attack. We'll have to move her body later."

Sam gently pushed my shoulder. I backed out of the doorway, raced to the computer, and pulled the thumb drive from it. I looked up to see Sam watching me. As I put it into my purse, his eyes never left mine. Still, he didn't say a word.

Just then, Sophia's boss moved to the doorway. He took several steps toward me. In a threatening voice, he shouted,

"You, whatever your name is, don't say a word to anyone about this. If this leaks out, I'll know where it came from, and I will make you wish you had never been born. Everything has to look normal, understand?"

I nodded my head while tears trailed down my face. "What about tomorrow? Am I supposed to still come into the office?" I whispered in a hoarse voice.

"When are you scheduled for the Purple Passion Lounge?"

"Not until next Monday, for training."

"Then show up for work that day. Now get the hell out."

Sam walked me to my car and said, "You need to be careful. For God's sake, don't say anything about this. Here's my number. Call me within a day or two, and I'll tell you what's happening with Sophia."

In gratitude, I grabbed his arm with shaking hands. "Thank you, Sam."

He nodded his head and gently guided me toward my car. "Drive carefully now."

As if I could….

CHAPTER 18

I annoyed every driver on the road, and they let me know I had by honking their car horns and freely waving their middle finger at me. Some called me names, even a few I had never heard before, as I crawled along the roads trying to make my way home. I was in a daze after all that had happened. I kept thinking how fortunate I was not to meet Brian at Sam's. I couldn't have done it and pretended nothing was wrong.

When I got home, Sweet Pea was glad to see me. As I picked her up and held her close, I began to cry earnestly. Poor Sophia. Was there anything I could have done to prevent her death? I knew I had to let that thought go or go crazy.

I made my way to the kitchen and poured myself a stiff vodka. Then I headed to the couch, with Sweet Pea trailing close on my heels. I could tell she sensed my sadness. As I sat there, my thoughts ran wild. I certainly had managed to get so deeply entrenched in the murders of Melissa and Sally and now the natural death of Sophia that I couldn't see any way out. All this within eight days! I decided that I had no choice but to ride this horse until the end. What other option did I have? I gave a deep sigh and sniffled some more about my difficulty.

Suddenly, I sat straight up, remembering I hadn't called Brian—something I wasn't about to do now. I wasn't able to talk to anyone, much less him. I hunted down my purse, which I had let drop as soon as I had come through the door. I grabbed my telephone and sent him a quick text. I said I wasn't feeling well and we would talk in the morning. I put my phone back on vibrate and tossed it into my purse.

I moaned and wondered what I was going to do. That's when I heard pounding on the front door. Thinking it had to be Brian, I thought, Just go away!

Sweet Pea began barking uncontrollably and wouldn't stop. I decided to ignore both Sweet Pea and the knocking at the door. I remained still and quiet in my bedroom, trying to compose myself.

Suddenly, I heard the door swing open and crash against the wall. "What is going on?" I yelled as I headed down the stairs. At the bottom of the stairs, I stood in shock with my mouth open. It wasn't Brian at all but rather two men in black masks.

"What do you want?"

"Awright, lady, just give it to me."

"Give you what?"

"You know what as well as I do!"

"I have no idea what you're talking about!"

The first one said to the other, "Grab the dog! Maybe she'll talk then."

"My dog doesn't know what you want, either," I retorted stupidly.

"Haha. We have a live one here. I like a feisty lady."

"Feel free to search for whatever you want, but I can tell you I don't have whatever you're looking for."

Sweet Pea began to twist and turn in the intruder's arms until he was forced to let her go. She headed out the front door as fast as she could, barking so much that my nearest neighbor stepped outside and called, "Rosalie, is everything okay?"

The man who stood closest to me swung his arm toward me. That is the last thing I remember until I woke up with my neighbor fanning his arm above me. Ron was calling, "Rosalie, come back to us. You're okay now."

I sat up and could feel a bump rising on my forehead. I rose on one elbow and told my neighbor, "Ron, I'm fine. Honestly, I am. Please let me get up."

"Do you want me to call the police?"

That was the last thing I wanted, so I said, "No, Ron, thank you anyway. I'll contact them in a few minutes. Thanks so much for coming to my rescue."

"These kids today. Always looking for drug money, huh? Good thing Sweet Pea was on the alert. I'm glad I got here before any more damage could be done. Are you sure you're okay?"

As I nodded, he said, "Okay, if you're sure, I'll head back home then."

"Thanks again for everything."

"Sure thing," he said, and off he went.

I closed the door and secured it as best as possible since the intruders damaged the lock when they entered. I had no choice but to call a locksmith to change the locks as soon as possible.

Guess I better put stronger ones on all the doors," I mumbled. "Damn it, I need to remember to use my alarm system, which for some stupid reason, I seem to ignore."

I arranged with the locksmith to come, who said he'd be there within the hour. I lay down on my bed to rest. A few minutes later, I faintly made out my telephone vibrating in my purse, which I had brought upstairs after locking up the house to the best of my ability. Was this day never going to end? I reached for the phone and saw the call was from one of my close friends, Karen, from Boston. Suddenly, I was glad to answer.

"Hi, Rosie! I'm just checking in to see how everything is going. Nancy, Susannah, and I are getting excited to see you soon! It will be good to relax, unwind, and be naughty in Vegas like old times, right?"

Despite being close to tears, I laughed just hearing my dear friend's voice. Being "naughty" in Vegas meant shopping, shopping, and shopping—which was a far cry from what I was discovering being naughty in Vegas was all about.

We chatted some more about simple things. I didn't share any of what was happening with her, but Karen intuitively sensed something because her parting words were, "See you soon. Stay safe, my friend."

"From your lips to God's ears," I whispered. I smelled my grandmother's favorite perfume and knew she was there to help me.

CHAPTER 19

E arly the following day, Brian pounded on my door. When I opened it, he pushed in, swooped up Sweet Pea—who was prancing around his feet—and asked, "Just what the hell happened?"

"What do you mean?" I responded, dread filling me.

"My friend from the police department called me this morning to say that your neighbor wanted to file a complaint about two hoodlums looking for drug money in your neighborhood yesterday. He mentioned your name."

Damn. "Oh, that," I answered, relieved it wasn't about Sophia. "Oh, no big deal. It's taken care of now anyway."

"What do you mean it's taken care of? How come you didn't file a complaint, Rosie? I don't like this one little bit."

"No worries. I had new locks installed, and I will be using my security system from now on."

"That's all fine and well, but that won't stop someone from entering if they want to. You know that, right?"

"Well ..."

"Well, nothing. Things are getting more complicated with these two murders we're investigating. I'm worried about you, and I want you to pull out NOW!'

"I can't do that, Cowboy. You know I can't. I have commitments, and I'm going to keep them."

"What commitments are you talking about?"

"Monday, I start at the Purple Passion Lounge, and I promised Sophia I would be there," I answered with a lump in my throat.

"That may have to change ...."

"Nothing's going to stop me from doing that," I interrupted in a determined voice, knowing full well that my life had been threatened to make me keep everything "normal" and show up for work as scheduled.

"We need to talk, Rosie. I meant it when I said that things were getting complicated. Things are not what we may have thought. I couldn't meet you last night because I was tailing Tony Angelo to see what I could find out. There's more going on at the Purple Passion Lounge than getting clients drunk and fleecing them out of their money. I don't want you involved."

"Well, I'm afraid that is not your decision. I will begin working at the Purple Passion Lounge on Monday, and that's that."

"Damn it, Rosie; you need to do what I say this time!"

"Listen, Cowboy, who do you think you're talking to? I don't take orders from you or anyone. I have made up my mind about this, and nothing is going to change it."

"I thought this would happen," he said with a sigh. "You're maddening. I knew you'd be too stubborn to change your mind, so I have a proposal for you. I want you to consider my offer, and I won't accept any excuse from you for not doing what I ask." He carefully emphasized the last word. "I want to hire a personal bodyguard for you."

"Well, we'll see …."

After Brian left, I needed to clear my head, so I took Sweet Pea for a walk in the large dog park near my house. I thought about Brian and his proposal, so I wasn't watching where I was going. I bumped into a man who was as surprised to see me as I was to see him. Instantly, I recognized him as one of the men who had broken into my house. Before I knew what was happening, he grabbed me around the neck and pulled me toward him. He whispered in my ear, "Give it to me!"

"Give you what?" I hollered, angered at being held captive and not knowing precisely what he wanted. Was it the money? The coded notes? The thumb drive? Sweet Pea began growling and barking, jumping up on him. She yelped when he kicked her into the air. That did it for me! No one was ever allowed to hurt my dog. A surge of adrenaline surged through my body. I surprised him with my sudden twisting, which I had learned in karate class, and I landed a swift kick to his knee. That caused him to twist in pain and lose his balance. As he writhed in pain, I brought my foot down on his groin. The expression "Never kick a man when he is down" didn't apply in this case. I bent over him and whispered, "Don't you ever hurt my dog again! I don't have what you think I do, so leave me alone, or I'll…."

A woman had heard Sweet Pea's barking and yelping and had come running as fast as she could. "What's happening?" she screamed as she raced toward me, out of breath. "Want me to call the police?"

Once the man heard that, he painfully forced himself up to his knees and, with pleading eyes, hoarsely whispered, "Okay, lady, I'll leave you alone. Just don't call the cops. If you do, I'm dead meat." He half crawled and ran away as I stood there in shock. I certainly didn't want anyone calling the police. I knew that would entail nothing good. What was I going to do?

"What was that all about?" the woman asked, breathless.

I knew she couldn't have heard his whispers, so I said, "That jerk was upset because I bumped into him, and he took it out on Sweet Pea. Can you imagine that?"

After she left, I stood there trying to understand what had just happened. I started to shake as adrenaline began to drain from my body. What worried me most was that I had enjoyed the physical aspect of my encounter with the man. Being able to defend myself and overpower a man that large was more than satisfying. It went beyond a judo class with disciplined steps and parrying. I had been fighting for a cause and had won.

Feeling so jubilant about my part in what had happened made me feel proud, yet injuring a person wasn't anything I "should" be proud of, was it?

My thoughts returned to the man I had run into. Why was he even here? Had he been following me all along, or had someone tipped him off about my whereabouts?

It was time to call Brian to tell him I'd made up my mind about his proposal. When I punched his number, his phone rang, but there was no response. It left me no choice but to leave a message. "Hey, Cowboy, give me a call, please."

I expected him to call me immediately, but my phone remained silent for the rest of the day. Something was up all right, something bigger than my incident, for he would have called me by now, wouldn't he?

When Brian called me later, he hurriedly said, "My friend in the police department called me late this afternoon to give me a lead on a story. They found an older man badly beaten and nearly dead in the parking lot near PUP's office. They found his wallet a few feet away from him. All his money was still there. They have identified him as Samuel Jenkins. Right now, he's in a coma at the hospital and unable to talk. Do you know anything about him?"

My heart fell, and my eyes watered as I answered, "I met him at PUP. He's responsible for inspecting the cars to ensure they are up to snuff before their owners join as drivers."

I paused, trying to remember my last conversation with Sam. I wouldn't be sharing that with Brian. I had promised not to say anything to anyone about my last day at PUP—a memory that would remain with me forever—and I wasn't about to break that promise. "Sam knew my grandmother when I was very young. After he saw me at PUP, he told me that it was because of my hair that he recognized me. That's all I know about him."

I could sense Brian biting back a chuckle when he heard the comment about my hair. There was no doubt my hair was a dead giveaway, with its long flyaway curls that sought freedom from anything that tried to contain them. My hair makes it difficult not to draw attention to myself.

My stomach began to churn at the vision of Sam lying on the hard pavement with no one there to help him. I made a slight choking sound as I held back tears.

Brian said with concern, "Rosie, you've got to give up working at the Purple Passion Lounge now. It's *not* safe."

"We don't know whether there's any connection between what happened to Sam and anything to do with the Purple Passion Lounge. So, I can promise you this—I will be there on Monday, and no one, not even you, can stop me."

There was a long pause. Brian was dismayed at my refusal to stop my part in the investigation. When he finally spoke, he said, "At least you'll take me up on my proposal, right?"

"Yes, I will."

"Good. Mike will be there in the morning. That will give you both several days to get acquainted. He's a really good guy and very professional."

"Okay," I answered meekly. It would be interesting to have a boyfriend again—even a pretend one. Mike was the man Brian hired to be my bodyguard and play the new love in my life.

As I picked up the tarot cards on the coffee table, they fell out of my hands, and I knelt to pick them up. Most had stayed together, and gathering them in one swoop was easy, pushing them together quickly. One fell out, and as I reached for it, I saw it was the Death card. I put it back into the deck with certainty that I wouldn't go to the hospital tomorrow to see Sam. It was already too late.

CHAPTER 20

S ecretly, I felt relieved Mike would stay with me for the next few days as my protector and "boy-friend" per Brian's orders. I became increasingly curious to learn more about Brian and what he was all about. Why did Brian have the authority to tell others what to do? Just who was he? I would know soon enough, as we were meeting at nine o'clock sharp. Our meeting would be difficult as we came clean about what was happening. I dreaded it as much as I would be relieved to share what I knew. I just needed to be strong … little did I realize how strong.

Brian came swinging into the house, all businesslike, with a slight frown. He almost didn't stop to take the time to bend down and pat Sweet Pea, who was bouncing at his feet. "Where's Mike?"

I pointed to the living room, where Mike sat with a cup of coffee I had made for him. Brian went in to speak with him. I could just make out what he was saying. "Listen, Mike. Now that I'm here, I need you to run that errand we discussed, okay?"

"Sure, boss," he responded good-naturedly.

"Rosie, where are your car keys? Hand them to me, please."

"Here you go," I responded, tossing them to Brian.

He gave them to Mike, saying, "Thanks for everything. I appreciate you stepping in."

Mike responded teasingly, "You have no idea how much fun this will be."

Brian looked surprised and annoyed at the same time and pointed to the front door. At that, Mike drained his cup, made his way toward me, and—play-acting the role of boyfriend—gave me a goodbye hug and went out the door. Brian looked unhappy, and Sweet Pea was beside herself to think she was losing an admirer. She barked in annoyance. I picked her up to keep her quiet and stared at Brian. "Are you ready?" I asked, dreading the moment I'd unveil what I'd been hiding from him.

"Absolutely."

"Let's go into my office."

"Sounds good to me."

After I had settled into one of the two club chairs facing my desk while Brian settled in the other, he looked sternly at me. "I know that you are hiding something from me, Rosie. I need to know everything now! No fooling around!"

"I promise to share what I have, but first, I need to know who you are. People are answering to you, and you don't seem like your average news reporter. What's really going on?"

Although I knew what it was, I wanted to hear it from Brian himself. He hesitated, obviously wondering whether he should blow his cover. He looked at me and said nothing for a minute or so. Then he must have decided he could trust me. He sat down hard in the soft armchair, leaned forward, and pushed his hand through his auburn curls.

"If we're working together, you need to know more. What I tell you is in strict confidence, of course. I'm doing undercover work because we believe this group connected with the Purple Passion Lounge is involved with drugs in a big way, and we're getting ready to split it wide open. We have been following them for more than a year. We know that something huge is going down soon. Yes, we're interested in finding Melissa's and Sally's killer or killers, something I know you want. I want it too. But our priority is the drug bust. That has to come first. Do you understand?"

"Who do you work for?' I asked as curiosity built. "Who is the 'we'?"

"It's a long story." He sighed. "It's hard to explain," he said, procrastinating, "and somewhat hard to believe." After a long pause, he continued. "After my sister died, I was contacted by a man who'd read about what'd happened in the news. He had a similar story about his own sister, and that hadn't ended well for her, either. He wanted to make up for his sister's attacker getting away scot-free by helping me do whatever was needed to bring my sister's attacker to justice. Most important, he was willing to pay me whatever amount of money it took for me to do so. Before too long, I was successful in helping put away my sister's attacker for a very long time."

"Tell me more," I encouraged.

"Strangely, I've never met this man in person, and I don't know who he is. However, he was so impressed with what

I'd done that he wanted me to continue working for him now and then to help solve different cases that interested him. He has the power and unlimited money to pull some strings. He's the one who arranged for me to get the job at the station."

"Wow, that's unbelievable."

"It is because of him I've also been able to set up my own investigative business in Boston. So you know, Mike is my business partner. There are others on staff besides the two of us."

"I'm not sure I fully understand. So what exactly is this guy's interest in the drug bust?"

Brian looked a little sheepish. "I don't know, and I don't ask. As long as everything is on the up and up, that's all that matters to me."

"It sounds like you're his Robin Hood for hire," I mumbled.

Brian chuckled with pleasure. "I guess," is all he said. "Do you understand why it's so important for me to bring the drug bust to a close? Even though I think you should opt out of everything, I know you won't. Are you okay working with us on that?"

"Yes, for sure. I believe it's all tied together with Melissa and Sally's situations, don't you?"

He nodded in agreement.

I would see to it that Melissa and Sally wouldn't be forgotten. As I sat there taking it all in, yes, there was a lot to be said about that. I recalled a saying my grandmother used—"Everything in its own time." However, as a shiver of premonition that something big was coming to a head overwhelmed me, I snapped at Brian, "You couldn't have filled me in on this sooner?"

"Would it have made a difference?"

"Maybe," I responded. "Who else knows?" I asked, "Does your boss at the station know about you and what you do?"

"No, and we don't want him to. He seems far too interested in squashing any new info concerning the murders or anything to do with all the drugs so readily available. He has refused to let me do any news reporting or expose it in any way."

Ruminating, I said, "It seems odd that he hasn't caught on that you aren't a real reporter, especially when he sees you on television."

"And sees something besides how handsome I am?" he asked in jest.

"Well, each time I've seen you on TV, you don't seem to have much to say. It's usually very hurried, without much meat to it."

Instead of being offended, Brian rolled his eyes and laughed out loud. "To be honest, my boss thinks I am the worst reporter he has ever had—as well as the biggest pain in the ass, what with me hounding him about the murders and drugs. That's why he's been giving me all the little non-happenings around town—all that reporting that no one else wants to do—which has turned out to be a blessing. It gives me time to do my own investigating."

"Hmm. Well, that's good then, isn't it?"

Brian nodded in agreement and looked at me expectantly. "Well? Now it's your turn, Rosie."

"Are you good at solving puzzles?"

"Not too bad. Why?"

"I have something to show you."

Brian's eyes widened. "What is it?"

"Wait here. I'll be right back."

Earlier, I had removed Melissa's package from my special hiding place, grabbed the mysterious notes from the bag, and taken them into my office to make copies. I then placed the copies in my hiding place as a backup in case I needed them. I debated whether to remove the money from the envelope before giving it to Brian. I decided I wouldn't and placed Melissa's full envelope in my sock drawer to wait for Brian to arrive.

As I hurried downstairs after grabbing the package, my heart beat a mile a minute. I could feel my face flush with excitement and nervousness. I handed Brian the package and watched his face as he opened the envelope and saw the money. He poked further and pulled out the envelope written to Melissa's mother. The notes must have stuck again, for I couldn't see them in his hand or lap. As I went to say something to him, he peeked inside the envelope and pulled out the notes. He was pissed. "What the fuck? What are these? Where did these come from?"

I stood there saying nothing, not knowing where to begin.

"God damn it, Rosie, you've been holding out on me—on all of us. Tell me about everything right now!" he demanded with fury.

"Okay," I answered stiffly, feeling guilty that I hadn't trusted him initially. "Well, I suggest you start by reading the notes from Melissa to me."

I caught him up on everything but what had happened to Sophia at PUP. My life, and perhaps his too, would be in greater danger should that leak out and Sophia's boss find out.

"Let's go over this again. I have to know every little detail, understand? No more holding out on me."

I hated to be in the wrong, and I was getting angry. What had I known about Brian before I got into this with him? "Just a minute. Back up, Mr. B. B."

At hearing his initials spit out, he blushed, looking uncomfortable. "Don't call me that name again, hear?" he demanded through gritted teeth.

"I will if I have to get your attention, Mister Cowboy! You need to be reminded that I met you just a few days ago, so how was I to know you could be trusted with all of this?"

I was furious with Brian. He was angry with me as well. He rose from his chair with his arms crossed in front of him and glared at me. We were at a standstill. There was an undeniable current of electricity between us, and it took my breath away. I knew he could feel it too. He started to reach his hand out to me, but instead of letting him pull me into his arms, I took several deep breaths. I stepped back and announced, "I'm going to get a cup of coffee. Would you like one too?"

He was confused and upset and didn't respond right away. He sat back down and replied stiffly, "That would be nice. Thank you very much."

When I returned, I sat across from him and asked, "Do you think Melissa was also dealing drugs?"

"Probably, don't you?"

"No, I don't. I can't explain why I feel that way, but I believe she's innocent of that. It doesn't make sense that she'd be heavily involved in dealing drugs and big money and suddenly become a simple PUP driver. Especially since she wasn't using drugs herself."

"Not everyone who deals drugs is a user, you know."

"True. But it doesn't add up for Melissa."

"Maybe she was transporting the drugs. Who knows? What about Sam? Look at what happened to him. Maybe he's part of it. You said he was the one who inspected the cars. He could've made a spot for the drugs to hide, couldn't he?"

"I suppose," I responded, with no conviction.

"By the way, we have secured Melissa's car, and nothing seems out of line there, so maybe Sam is clear as well. Speaking of him, let's check with the hospital and find out if he's awake enough to talk to us."

"There's no point," I responded with sadness. "It's too late."

"How do you know?" he responded with some irritation. "I haven't heard anything about that."

"I just do," I said weakly.

At that moment, the phone rang for Brian. He listened and looked at me oddly. "Okay, then. Thanks for the call."

"You're right, Rosie. Sam died early this morning."

We spent most of the day reviewing and discussing what we didn't know. We marked a few items on the whiteboard. "Did you ever interview the old lady who heard something the night Sally was killed?" I asked.

"Yeah. She only heard scuffling sounds. She never saw anyone that night. She identified Tony, though, as someone who came to Sally's condo off and on. But that's not unusual since they were family and in the lounge business together."

"What about Melissa's boss? Anything new on him?"

"That's where you will come in handy by working at the lounge. We're relying on you to give us as much information as you *safely* can. No taking chances for you, Rosie; do you understand?"

I nodded yes and looked away. I would do whatever was necessary to put the drug dealers behind bars, whether it was safe.

"I have several men scheduled to take turns as customers at the Purple Passion Lounge when you're working there, so please let me know your schedule as soon as possible. Are you sure you are going to be okay working there? Do you still want to go through with all this?"

"Absolutely. I don't know why you keep asking me that. How often do I need to tell you you can count on me? I'm in this to the end," I snapped.

"Okay, okay. You don't have to bite my head off."

"Then stop asking me." After a minute or two, I leaned toward Brian and said, "Sorry. I'm just a little on edge."

"So are we all. What time do you go to work Monday for training?"

"I have to be there by 10."

Brian nodded his head. "Okay then. I'll have each man who'll be there undercover as a guest ask you if your name is Linda. That way, you will know who they are."

Brian looked at his watch and started to get up. "Mike should be back sometime soon."

I noticed dark circles under his eyes as he stared at me. I knew he was worried and probably had not been sleeping much lately. As he stood, so did Sweet Pea, lying at his feet. She stared at him and wagged her tail, pleading with him to pay attention to her. Honestly, I had to admire Sweet Pea, for she was straightforward in letting anyone know her desires. No games for her. There was something to be said about that.

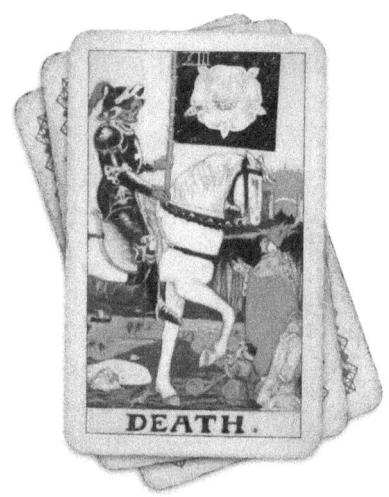

CHAPTER 21

Mike Williams was in his late 30s, maybe even early 40s, tall and handsome—and at 6′2″, a bit taller and broader than Brian. He had a full head of black hair, intense dark brown eyes, and tanned skin, which made him look like the outdoorsman he was. Although he and Brian were opposite in coloring, they had a similar air about them. They were sure in their ways, which caused others to look to them for leadership. They wouldn't take guff from anyone, which was comforting.

Mike settled in as if he were used to living here. It'd taken me a bit to relax with him because I wasn't used to sharing my space with anyone, something I hadn't done since Jeff died. However, I was still on edge from having a stranger in the house.

I looked around my house from a different perspective, from what might be Mike's viewpoint. I was pleased by how comfy the entire place seemed, even with some of the original valuable artwork and antiques my parents had collected worldwide. The nice thing for people entering was that they could sense right away it'd be more than okay to take off their shoes and curl up on the couch to relax, mainly because of the way I had utilized and mixed some of my parents' treasures in with my unique way of designing.

At suppertime, I poured myself a glass of wine. I offered Mike a beer, but he refused, saying he was on the job. I turned on the news to see whether anything new had happened. There was a small blurb about Sam, whose death was described as a robbery. Both Mike and I knew that wasn't true.

"God, Mike, it's amazing what gets on the news that isn't true with no one to call them on it. It's scary."

"You have no idea, doll."

"What do you think, Mike? Are we going to be able to catch these guys in the act and get them busted for dealing drugs?"

"Oh, we'll get them all right."

There wasn't anything else of any significance on the news, so I switched it off and put on soft music. I'd wondered whether Mike would tell me more about Brian's heartbreak. By now, I knew the woman who'd broken his heart was his sister, so I asked, "Was Brian's sister younger than he?"

"He told you about that?" he asked, somewhat surprised.

"Well, not everything. What happened?"

"She was younger than Brian. She attended one of the prominent colleges in Boston. In her second year there, she was attacked, raped, beaten very badly, and nearly died. She was ridiculed when she tried to bring charges against her attacker because 'she must have encouraged him in some way.' Others accused her of wanting revenge for something she had allowed to happen. The shame and accusations that others tossed her way were endless."

"Oh, my God!"

"The man who raped and beat her destroyed her. She never was the same. She became afraid of everything and hid in her condo from the outside world. She lost the reality of things around her. The rapist had taken away every ounce of her joy in living, and nine months later, she overdosed and died."

"How sad," I said with a heaviness in my heart. "Did you know her?"

"At the time, I was the policeman who found her. That's how I met Brian."

"I didn't know you used to be a policeman."

"A detective, actually."

We both were quiet, lost in our thoughts. I got up and went into the kitchen to organize something for us to eat. I made grilled cheese and tomato sandwiches—comfort food.

Afterward, Mike helped me clean up. Then I headed upstairs to read in bed. Mike would be sleeping in the guest room farthest from me so I could have more privacy. He'd also take over the couch at times when he became restless.

The following morning, we each did something on our separate computers. I looked at my tarot cards sitting on my desk and ignored them. I didn't want to know what might happen, especially if the Death card were to come up again.

Later, Mike and I went to the grocery store together, putting what we liked to eat into the cart. Mike wanted red meat, something I didn't eat too often. I filled the cart with vegetables and fruit. We grabbed the same coconut gelato in the frozen food section and bought four. I knew we gave the appearance of a happy couple, for we found ourselves laughing at our situation while others looked on with approval. I wondered if it would have been the same had it been Brian rather than Mike.

Later, I grilled the steaks outside with some asparagus, and we enjoyed dinner sitting on the patio together. I had a nice glass of pinot noir, while Mike refused any alcohol, again stating he was on the job. That brought me back to the reality of what was going on.

On the last night before I started at the Purple Passion Lounge, we watched the movie *Vegas Vacation,* and we both roared over the antics of Chevy Chase and his reaction to Wayne Newton's attraction to his wife. It was such fun to laugh like that again. I was grateful that Brian had insisted Mike be here to protect me. I was getting comfortable with having him around, which made me less tense. After the movie, I checked my watch and rose from the couch. I gathered Sweet Pea, nestled against Mike, and headed upstairs.

I fell into a deep sleep without dreams until 5:30, when Sweet Pea woke me up with kisses on my cheek. I felt disoriented until I remembered today was my first day at the Purple Passion Lounge. I sat straight up in bed, and as I reviewed everything that led to that day, my head began to whirl. I lay back in bed, closed my eyes, and meditated.

Twenty minutes later, I reluctantly rose and headed into the bathroom to shower and get dressed. I wasn't sure what the dress code was for someone in my position there, so I slipped into a simple classic navy linen sleeveless dress. That would have to do.

At 9:30 a.m., I said goodbye to Sweet Pea and told Mike it was time for him to drive me to work. It wouldn't seem unusual for Mike (my "boyfriend") to be at my side. It also helped that many men his age often preferred dating a younger woman, so we didn't look out of place.

On the way to the lounge, Mike said, "Keep your eyes and ears open, and for God's sake, please be careful! Don't act interested in what everyone else is doing, either. Just be nonchalant."

"I've got it covered, Mike. I know what to do."

"And also," he continued, "you might want to …."

"Mike, if you don't quit now, I will ask you to stop the car and let me out. You are making me so nervous …."

"Sorry. You're right. Sorry."

Mollified by knowing he was concerned about me, I sat back in my seat and began to meditate to calm myself. I was extremely nervous about jumping into this new position without Sophia's guidance. I had no idea what to expect.

I took in everything about the building when we pulled into the Purple Passion Lounge. It was larger than I expected, and its appearance suggested that the wider section in the rear of the building didn't match the front; it looked like an addition. I was curious about that and made plans to check that out when I could. Both the front and sides of the building were covered with black glossy tiles, with a rounded front entrance protected by a large, extended, fancy porte cochere held up by white columns similar to those I equate with Southern mansions.

Along the curb was a black marquee sign with bright purple lettering alerting all of Las Vegas that this was the place to come if you wanted to see girls. Of course, Sally was in her renowned stance of tits and butt at the bottom right of the sign. The building reminded me of an older, somewhat gaudy restaurant past its prime. Yet, in its way, it still seemed elegant and rather charming. I scoffed at myself. We'd have to see just how charming it really was.

We parked the car, and Mike walked me to the front door, which was locked. I rang the bell, and I could hear footsteps hurrying toward us. As the door cracked open, a pretty girl peeked out and gave me a questioning look as she looked at me curiously. I said, "Hi, my name is Rosalie. The new girl? I'm supposed to take over the front desk."

"Ah, yes. Rosalie, right? Come on in."

As she opened the door wider, she noticed Mike standing there. She asked, "Who's this?" as she looked him up and down, taking in all of him.

"Oh, this is my boyfriend, Mike."

"Well, you'll have to return, Mike; it isn't time to open. We're closed from 4 in the morning until 4 in the afternoon so the cleaning people can get everything in order, and we can get some sleep." She seemed to be teasing him.

The girl turned toward me. "By the way, I'm Cindy, though some call me Sweet Thing. I'll be the one showing you around today. Come on in."

Mike stood his ground until I lightly kissed him. I could feel Cindy watching us. As the door closed behind us, she shoved me in a friendly manner and teasingly said, "Honey, you'll never keep that man that way. They always want more than a stodgy kiss."

"I suppose you're right."

"You know it, girl."

I just rolled my eyes and followed along.

CHAPTER 22

A fter Cindy and I entered the Purple Passion Lounge through the heavy double doors, we were in a bright, short hallway that led to another set of double doors. We opened them and entered the large greeting area, welcoming and glowing with incandescent light. Mirrored walls and marble floors were everywhere we walked, with gray tones giving the appearance of eloquence and richness, even if it was a bit tacky. I had to smile, for it seemed more like the reception area of a high-end corporation. Oh, my.

I spotted the large curved desk where I assumed I'd be working. It was close to the entrance of what I thought must be the bar. Across from the desk was a sizeable one-way window that allowed us to see outside and kept those out from seeing in. I watched Mike drive away.

As we walked past the area where I'd be working, I spotted two plush chairs behind the desk, which also held a computer and other things I'd need. The front of the desk was raised about 18 inches and served as a small countertop, providing privacy. As they walked by, it would block the patrons' view of everything on the desk.

I expected the bar area to be beyond the desk. Instead, we rounded the corner and entered another beautiful, long hallway. Along the way, there were several wide-open rooms with heavy drapes serving as doors that could partially close off the area when they weren't tied back. Depending on the size of the room, each contained one or two leather couches, matching chairs, and various café tables and chairs. Although the rooms were tastefully done, I didn't even want to think about what had happened there.

What I thought would be a simple bar area was so much more. My eyes were drawn to the curved bar with plush, heavy stools taking up the entire wall on the far side of the room. The shelves behind the bar were fully stocked with all varieties of liquor bottles. I couldn't imagine anyone asking for liquor that they wouldn't have on hand.

The ceiling was an enormous dropped ceiling, with all kinds of reflectors and lights that focused on a single pole on a raised platform, where I imagined the girls taking turns dancing for their guests.

The main bar had expensive-looking small mahogany café tables and plush cushioned chairs, but everything was cheapened by black walls and bright purple touches that reminded me of the clownish look I had seen on their website. The lights were kept dim to allow some privacy— but not enough to completely take away the possibility and fun of becoming a voyeur to what was happening at the next table. I knew about lap dances but had never seen or participated in one. I tried not to go there in my mind's eye.

Cindy had been continuously talking to me, and I'd not been listening, so I asked her, "What was that you said, Cindy?"

"I'm showing you all this because to get to the back area where we can eat and take a break, we have to go through this room. Other than that, you are not supposed to be in here, okay?"

"Sure. No problem."

"Great. Now follow me, and I'll show you our employee lounge area and bathrooms."

I followed her, with excitement building in my stomach. It would be exciting to be a part of discovering and taking down whoever killed Melissa and Sally. Intuitively, I knew both deaths were connected to the people here, but I didn't know how yet. I needed not to act naïve and play my role here with more aplomb. "Cindy? What is the dress code for me here?"

She looked me up and down. A look of amusement crossed her face. "Well, for starters, you look like you're going to court or something. Very vanilla. Whether you wear a dress or pants doesn't matter, but I think you'll want the top to show a little cleavage, you know?"

After a look at my face, she added, "You don't have to dress like the girls or be too provocative, but a little bit helps."

"Just go with the flow," I muttered to myself. "If you want to do this job right, follow what she said." I sighed. Who'd have thought I'd be working in a gentlemen's club in Las Vegas?

Beyond the bar, we went down another hallway to the employee lounge. There were offices along one side. Toward the end of the hallways was the employee lounge. It was surprisingly lavish, with all stainless steel appliances and a cappuccino maker. There were full-sized lockers along the back wall, where we could put our coats, purses, and whatever else we could fit in. Each locker had a combination lock.

"This locker here will be yours. We have a new lock for you to use, and you can put in whatever code you want. I'll show you how it works."

I nodded and smiled at her. My mind was elsewhere because of all the visions of past happenings coming to me. I would have to block them to concentrate on what Cindy was telling me. Right now, I doubted I could even find my way back to the front of the building without her help.

After setting up the new lock, I stowed my purse inside. Cindy began to open and close the cabinets and refrigerator and point out different things in the kitchen. "We always have coffee available, so help yourself. The cream is right here in the refrigerator. We have soup and some other things in the cabinets. Help yourself to anything in this cabinet; the other cabinet is for whatever you want to bring to eat or drink. Just mark it with your name, or it will be gone! Capisce?"

I laughed and said, "Got it."

Cindy looked at me and smiled. "I think I'm going to like you."

"I'm going to like you too." There was something about Cindy that was soft and loving, not at all what I was expecting. I wondered whether we would find ourselves on the same side down the road.

CHAPTER 23

C indy walked me further to the back end of the main building, the square section I'd first noticed when Mike and I had driven in earlier. The closer we got to it, the more I could smell chlorine. "Is this what I think it is?" I asked Cindy.

"Yep, you guessed it. I'm telling you, we have everything here."

"The question is, do you *do* everything here?" I paused, not knowing how she would respond. That had rolled off my tongue before I realized what I had said.

Cindy just stared at me for a moment, then burst out laughing. "The hell with calling you Rosalie. I'm going to call you Rosebud for short."

I wasn't happy with my new name, but I would go along with it if I had to. We both looked at each other and laughed. Then Cindy opened the door, and we entered the heated pool area, skirted by cabanas. It was stunning. It appeared more like the old Roman baths, mainly because of the motif carried throughout the room.

"This area is for the higher-paying customers only. We never get to use it for recreation; we don't want to. It even has a separate entrance."

"It sure is a gorgeous space."

"The only thing I haven't shown you are the private sleeping quarters for the bosses and some off-limits offices. Other than that, what do you think?"

"Well, it's certainly more elegant than I'd thought. It's very nice and upscale. A nice surprise."

"Oh, my God, I forgot to show you my favorite room—the kitchen! It's located right to the left of the bar area, and we have a fabulous chef. And guess what? You can order from the menu for your break."

"I'd love to see it. Lead the way!"

The kitchen was every chef's dream. It was all stainless steel, with everything a chef could want. It had a large walk-in refrigerator and what looked like a large walk-in freezer half hidden behind the fridge. There was a long stainless prep table in the center of the room. Against the farthest wall was a top-of-the-line commercial oven with a six-burner stovetop, and there were also two separate ovens set away from the first stove. The arrangement was perfect, with a work triangle between the sink, refrigerator, freezer, and stove. My heart skipped a beat just seeing the perfection of it all.

I had barely taken notice of the man who had his back to us when we first stepped into the kitchen. Now he turned around and greeted us with enthusiasm. "Sweet Thing, my love, what delicious flower have you brought me?"

Cindy approached him, and they blew air kisses near each cheek. "Romano, this is Rosebud."

I blushed and corrected her. "Rosalie."

He stepped away from me while still holding onto my hands. "No, my sweet. You are a rosebud. Rosebud it is."

I smiled. Romano pulled me toward him, gave me two air kisses, and whispered in my ear, "My real name is John, but it wasn't fancy enough, so I renamed myself Romano after the cheese." Then he laughed at himself with delight. I fell in love with him at that moment. His eyes twinkled, and he looked me up and down. "Oh, darling, you must do something with those clothes. They do nothing for you!"

I could feel myself blush, and he immediately came to my aid. "Don't worry, Rosebud. Just go to Louie's and tell him I sent you. He'll know what to do. Do you know where it is?"

I shook my head.

"No? Right on Sahara Avenue, just beyond Jones." I still looked confused.

"No worries. I'll give Louie a call and tell him to expect you. When do you want to go? Tomorrow maybe? Around 10?"

Why not? I thought. "Sure. That'd be great. Thanks, Romano."

"Anything for you, darling."

"It was nice meeting you, Romano. I … "

"Sit, sit!" he ordered. "You can't leave now. I will do my famous scrambled eggs for my two special beauties, and you can't miss this, right, Cindy?"

Cindy nodded in agreement. "Romano's right. You'll want to stay put."

Romano had pulled out two metal stools from beneath the prep table. We dutifully sat and watched him work.

On a shelf above the prep table was a section filled with different seasonings, fresh-cut herbs, and other delights I didn't recognize in small glass bowls. He pulled out what he wanted and mixed everything into a bowl. Then, he tossed it all into the sizzling skillet with a grand flourish. He flipped the eggs only twice, creating a more well-done exterior and a slightly cheesier, gooey center.

I was practically drooling by the time he put my plate before me. In typical fashion, I swooned and made pleased sounds with each bite. Romano was watching me with pleasure. "Ah, Rosebud, a girl after my heart! Perfecto, huh?"

With my mouth stuffed, I could only nod. My God, these were the best eggs I'd ever had. I looked at Cindy, who enjoyed them as much as I was. She winked at me and said, "Delish."

We said goodbye to Romano with air kisses and promises to return. Cindy pulled me along. "I hope we're not late. Bertha is filling in, and she'll be the one who'll explain the front desk to you. She can be a bitch. We call her Mama, by the way. Let's hurry!"

We ran through the bar and down the wide hallway we had come through before. We arrived out of breath in the reception area and came face-to-face with a large, unattractive woman who was unhappy we were late.

Cindy said, "Sorry to keep you waiting, Mama." Then, using my formal name, she added, "This is Rosalie. She will take over the front desk for the first shift, 4 to 10 p.m."

Mama just eyed me and said nothing. She moved away from us and headed to the desk area, expecting us to follow.

Cindy tapped me on the shoulder and whispered, "See you later, Rosebud. Mine's the second shift, so I'll be back in time for it. See you later. Good luck," she added with a roll of her eyes.

I looked at Mama, who had turned to make sure I had followed her. I hurried to her side. She seemed to know the routine well, and it wasn't hard to catch on. It was straightforward, like any typical restaurant listing reservations on a computer. Besides the reservations, there was simply an entrance fee for the guest to pay, allowing them into the bar area, where the girls could upsell them on activities. The girls would be the ones to bring their guests' bills to the register, where I would either collect the money or charge their cards. Most of the clients used cash.

Interestingly, I wouldn't have to worry about punching in a category for payment for different activities because the bookkeeper would do that later from the slips the girls handed in. The bookkeeper would then enter each slip into her computerized bookkeeping program. The different codes the girls wrote down on the slips would tally their portion of the money due to them according to the activity. Not a great way to do business, but again, I was here only as the receptionist. The program was passcode-protected and wasn't even on my computer. Is that how Melissa had come up to the $23,345? She must have been swamped.

Mama caught my attention when she said, "Now, about PUP ...."

"Yes?"

"When the girls ask for a driver for their guest, they will tell you where they will be dropped off—at their hotel or wherever. You push this button on the telephone and record the message in the phone's handset; it will send a text. Then, you're done. One of the drivers will be here to pick up the passenger. You won't be alone. A security guard will always be here, and we have a security system that watches you and everyone else." She pointed to the ceiling, and I could see the same type of cameras used in the casinos.

"Did Cindy show you all around?"

"Yes, she did."

"Well, then, that's it for the day. Come back tomorrow, and I'll start you out on your shift until you feel comfortable. Go get your purse or whatever else you brought with you," she commanded briskly. "Do you need a ride?"

"No, I'll call my boyfriend. He'll pick me up."

For some odd reason, she seemed relieved to hear I had a boyfriend. What was that all about?

I got a bit lost on my way to the break room. When I got to the bar area, I saw the same man with the funny hairstyle I had seen with Sally that day we had met at the Bellagio. He was talking with Mama. When she saw me, she called me over. "Rosalie, this is Johnny. He's one of the people who'll be helping out in the front."

Worried that he might recognize me, I stuttered a response, "N..n..nice to meet you, Johnny."

"Yeah," he responded, not at all interested in me.

I left them and made my way to the break room. I called Mike to pick me up and wondered again, What the hell are you doing here, Rosie girl?

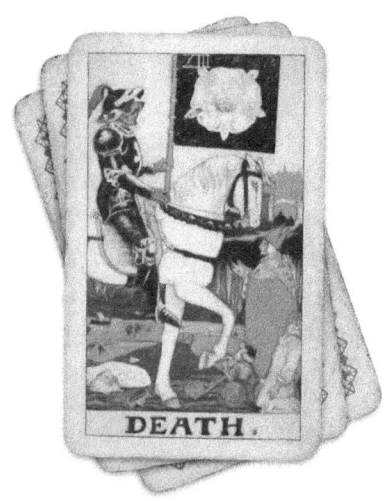

CHAPTER 24

Mike was happy to see me but not as delighted as Sweet Pea was. She bounced around in the car ... always pleased about the destination, not the journey. I pushed her aside so I could get in and sit down. She immediately sat on my lap and began licking my face. Mike just looked at us and smiled. "How was it?"

"Oh, my God—have you ever been in there?"

His face turned pink. He said, "Yeah, I scouted the area the other day with Brian."

"Then there isn't much to say. It's quite a place, isn't it?"

"Amazing, actually. Fancier than any of the others, for sure."

"Oh?"

He turned away from me and said, "Yup."

We arrived home in time to see my neighbor Ken, standing outside his house, poking at his plants. As soon as he saw us pulling into the driveway, he headed over, hollering at us. When I opened my door and poked my head out, he said, "Hey there, Rosalie, just wanted to let you know I called the police about those thugs. They promised to be on the watch for them. Said they'd check out our entire neighborhood too."

When he realized there was another person in the car whom he hadn't seen through the tinted windows, he immediately straightened up. He focused his attention on Mike as he exited the driver's seat. "And who is this?" he asked protectively.

"Ken, this is Mike."

"Is he visiting?"

It was my time to blush. "He's staying with me for a while."

"Oh, I see," he said. He looked at me with disappointment. I knew he didn't believe in cohabitation unless you're married. He'd said as much when Jeff moved in before our wedding date. I wondered what he'd say if he learned I was working at the Purple Passion Lounge.

"I'll make sure she's safe," said Mike as he shook hands with Ken.

"All right, then," responded Ken, viewing Mike's size. "Just make sure you do." And off he went.

Mike looked at me with a smile. "Very protective of you, is he?"

"He's been my neighbor ever since I moved here. I think he's felt responsible for me since my grandmother died."

"Nice to know."

Once inside, I changed into jeans and a t-shirt. Then I began to look through my clothes. I had some lovely dresses and tops, but I had to admit they were pretty "vanilla," just as Cindy had described my dress. It would be interesting to see what Louie would pick for me tomorrow. Meanwhile, I pulled out a light gray silk dress with peek-a-boo sleeves. I'd air it out and wear it tomorrow unless Louie had something else that would work better.

Thanks to my parents and grandmother's management of my inheritance, I owned my house and had considerable money invested, so I didn't have financial worries. However, I was pretty careful with my money and didn't like flaunting it in any way. Louie might be disappointed by the amount of money I'd be willing to spend there. We'd see.

Sweet Pea had stuck close to me ever since I'd come home. Then, without a second's hesitation, she left me and began running down the stairs to the front door before I heard anything. Of course, it was most likely Brian who was standing there.

Mike had dutifully answered the door. As I descended the stairs, I watched them shake hands before Mike closed the door and got out of Brian's way, allowing him to enter. They were an interesting pair, all right. Even more interesting was Sweet Pea. She stood there looking between them, wondering whom to go to first. She solved her problem by jumping on the first one, then the other. Mike patted her once. Brian swooped down and picked her up, laughing as she planted kisses on his face.

They both turned as I came down the last few steps. Each looked up and gave me a wide smile. How handsome they were. My heart fluttered at their attention. I hadn't allowed that from any male since Jeff had died. Perhaps Cindy's nickname of Rosebud was, for me, appropriate. I felt myself begin to open up with the desire to live a more "normal" life—one that might include a man. To stop further thoughts, I smiled and asked, "Coffee, anyone?"

"Sure thing," answered Brian. "So, how'd it go today?"

I waited for Mike to respond. He said, "No, thanks. You fill Brian in. I'm going for a walk, okay?" he asked, looking at Brian.

"Sure, Mike. Scout the area out. See if there are any places where someone could hide and surprise us."

"Will do."

I began filling Brian in, leaving out my new nickname. That was something that neither Brian nor Mike needed to know. "Cindy is very nice, and I like her. I think she can be trusted if need be. She's the one who will follow my shift. By the way, my shift is from 4 to 10 p.m. I don't know the days I'll work permanently, but I'll train there tomorrow."

"Just let me know when you find out."

"Didn't you say you had seen the woman they called Mama when you were there before?"

"Is she the one who's big and fat?"

"Yes, and not very pleasant."

"That's David Masterly's wife. Isn't she a piece of work?"

"She's the one who was training me today."

"No kidding? I bet she wasn't too happy with you!"

"Why do you say that?"

"Well, just look at the comparison between you two …"

"Oooh," I sighed, pleased.

I went into my office and grabbed a piece of paper and a pen. I returned to where we were sitting at the table and drew what a slip from one of the girls looked like when she handed it to me. I explained everything to him. We each had another coffee and sat quietly, reviewing what I'd drawn.

Out of the blue, Brian asked, "Have you ever shot a gun before?"

"Not really. Once, when I was a kid, my father taught me how to shoot at tin cans in the field behind the house we used to own."

"Well, I think it's important you learn how. After all, you never know when it might come in handy. What about tomorrow? Do you have an hour or two before you go to work?"

"No, not really. I have an appointment at Louie's."

"Louie's on Sahara?"

"I guess. Why? Do you know it?"

"Know of it!"

"He's a friend of Romano, the chef at the lounge. He's going to help me dress in a style that's more appropriate for there."

"You're kidding, aren't you?"

"No, I'm not. Apparently, anyone in that position …"

"Hold on just a minute! You're not going to have to wear what the girls there do, are you?"

"Oh, for heaven's sake, Cowboy. What if I am?"

"You're impossible, do you know that?"

"Why do you care anyway?"

Brian rose from his chair and just stood there looking at me. Then Mike entered the kitchen and saw us glaring at each other. He asked, "What's up?"

"Nothing," I said. "Cowboy here is trying to boss me around."

"You?" asked Mike. He turned to Brian and laughed. "Don't even try!"

Brian's phone rang, and we heard him say, "Oh, shit! I'll be right there!" He turned to us, "Gotta go. That was the boss calling. Keep in touch."

As Brian was leaving, Mike turned to me with a grin. "Cowboy? You call Brian Cowboy? He's got to love that!" he added sarcastically. Then he followed Brian to the door to lock up after him.

I just smiled.

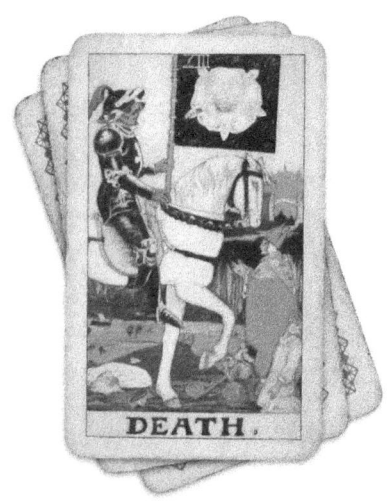

CHAPTER 25

T his morning was different from many others. I could smell fresh coffee brewing, a delightful smell that urged me to get up. I noticed Sweet Pea was already gone from the bed and assumed she was with Mike. I rolled over onto my back and basked in the feeling that all was cozy and safe. It was incredible what a difference having another person in the house could make. In this case, it was all good.

When I put on my robe, I realized I had forgotten to tell Brian that one of the people working the front area at the Purple Passion was the same one I had seen grabbing Sally at the Bellagio. The fact that he'd be working there with me was unsettling and would be until I could be sure he hadn't recognized me as the person meeting with Sally. At the time, I'd done the best I could to cover myself with my cap and hoodie, but only time would tell whether that had been good enough.

As I padded my way to the kitchen, it was nice to be greeted by Mike. He looked up with a big smile. Sweet Pea came forward, wiggling around and trying to get my full attention. "Ready for some of my famous eggs this morning?" asked Mike.

"That sounds wonderful, but first, I need a cup of java before thinking about anything else."

"Understood, madam. The chef will wait." We smiled at each other.

After a few sips of coffee, I asked. "Has Sweet Pea gone out yet?"

"All taken care of, madam. And she's fed as well."

"Gosh, thanks so much." Then I asked, "Good lord, what time is it?"

"Guess you needed the sleep because it's almost 8 o'clock."

"Oh, my! I've got to hurry! I've got to get to Louie's by 10."

"You've got two hours. Isn't that enough time?" he asked, completely perplexed.

"You men," I mumbled, shaking my head. "No lady likes to be rushed."

We left Sweet Pea home. If she could have stamped her feet in protest, she would have. It was bad enough when I left her behind, but now two people were doing so.

As we neared Louie's, I looked at Mike. I could tell he was amused at the idea of my going there. As we pulled up to the front of the store, I tried not to show my alarm. In the front window were some sexy outfits indicating practices I had only read about. I was about to ask Mike to drive us back home when Louie rushed out the front door.

"Welcome, Miss Rosebud! C'mon into my beautiful store!"

I looked at Mike and whispered, "Don't you dare say a word!"

Mike grinned. "Whatever you say, Rosebud."

Louie opened my door and held me by the arm like royalty. He led me into the store, calling over his shoulder, "Come back in two hours. She'll be done by then."

I wondered what he meant. I dutifully followed him. When he saw my reaction to viewing all the weird costumes and other items, he said, "Don't worry, my little flower. We are going into the back where all the beautiful things are. Do you know that I dress many of the stars?"

His statement made me more worried. Stars of what? Pornography?

As we passed by the checkout counter, we approached an elegant area with beautiful, soft music playing. The room was spacious and illuminated with lights that didn't glare like those in typical stores. Off to the side was an intimate setting with a small Victorian couch. In front of it were two parlor chairs covered in a gorgeous chintz rather than the usual velvet. They were stunning. In front of them was a glass coffee table with a beautiful silver tea service resting in the middle. I smelled a delicious mint scent and knew the tea was brewing just for us. There were dainty little treats on a silver plate and darling little napkins that I held up. They read, "I have enough clothes and shoes. I don't need to go shopping, said no woman ever." I had to smile, for there certainly was some truth in that.

Louie watched me. "A little humor … now, let's sit and have a cup of tea so I can get to know you. That helps me pick out the right clothes for you."

We talked for a while, and he asked a few strange questions: what season I liked best, what types of food, flowers, colors, etc., did I prefer? Louie seemed pleased with my answers. "I thought so," was all he said.

Then he left but returned with dresses, pants, and tops he had designed or picked from other designers. They were stunning and simple in design and fabric. And, of course, they were very sexy, but in ways that hinted at sexuality without showing outrageous amounts of skin. Each time I tried on a piece, I felt beautiful in ways I hadn't before. When it was time to say goodbye to Louie, I had tears in my eyes—and much less in my bank account. I thanked him profusely.

After air-kissing me, he whispered. "Remember, Rosebud, you truly are a beautiful flower." He pushed a piece of paper into my hand and said, "Go see my friend Richard. He'll do your hair. Tell him I sent you."

I was glowing. I hugged Louie again. "Thank you, dear Louie."

Mike watched us from the rear of the car as he waited to load all the bundles into the trunk. He had a strange look on his face. Instead of getting into the driver's seat, he came around and opened the door for me. I pretended he always did that for me and said in a regal voice, "Thank you."

My, I felt great! Thinking you're beautiful is good, but the feeling you are is even better!

CHAPTER 26

I slipped on the dress with the peek-a-boo sleeves that I had set out to wear today for work because, according to what I had learned from Louie, it would do.

I descended the stairs and called Mike, "It's time to go. Are you ready?"

He came around the corner and stopped, just observing me. "You look … very … beautiful."

"Thanks." Because of the look on his face, I asked, "Are you sure you're okay?"

"Yeah. Why'd you ask?"

"Nothing." I let it go. I didn't want to mention that no man since Jeff had ever looked at me that way, so this was something new. Hmmm.

"Okay, then," he said, clearing his throat. "Let's get moving. C'mon, Sweet Pea, you can ride with us."

When we arrived at the Purple Passion Lounge, many cars were in the parking lot beside the building. Mike drove past them to the grand entranceway underneath the porte cochere. Immediately, a valet came to open the door for Mike, and then he came around to open my door. Mike stepped out and came around to kiss me goodbye, this time with a resounding kiss on my cheek and a whisper—"I'll be back later."

I walked through the main door into the hallway leading to the reception area, where I could see myself in the mirror. My cheeks were flushed, and I looked happy.

I found my way into the bar area and could smell something delicious cooking. I peeked into the kitchen. There was Romano in all his glory, ordering two other people around. When he looked up and saw me, his smile broadened. "Ah, my little Rosebud!"

"Louie is a genius!" I exclaimed as we exchanged air kisses. "Romano, you are the best friend a girl could ever have. Thanks so much!"

"Not for everyone, my little flower, but for you, yes."

I found my way to the back, where I put my purse into my locker. I rewound my way to the front area, where Mama was waiting for me, none too pleased. I wondered whether that was the only expression she had. She was wearing a dress today and looked quite pretty despite what she had to work with, I thought unkindly. "Mama, you're looking very pretty today."

Mama tried to look unaffected by my comment, but she was pleased. "Aw right, then," she said dismissively. "Let me show you what we have here." She had saved some of the slips that needed to be recorded so we could do them together.

One of the girls stepped forward from the hallway and asked Mama, "Is this the new girl?"

Mama just nodded her head.

"Hi there, my name is Bambi. I work the early shift in the bar area. See you later!" Bambi was a beautiful girl who knew it. She was young, too young to be here, I thought. And too young to be letting anyone touch her in any scandalous way. I was pretty sure she was of legal age, though. Had to be to work here, right? And she acted as though it all was just a game. Oh, my.

Time passed quickly despite the majority of the clients staying a long time. Mostly, they weren't here to have a quick drink and be done with it. They were here for more than that. A few clients had made their own arrangements while still in the bar area and hailed a cab. I followed the girls' directions for calling PUP for transportation. They were then loaded into the cab, and off they went, a little lighter in the wallet, I was pretty sure. The alarming thing for me was that Johnny, the guy with the funny hair, waited around in the entrance area between clients' departures. He would stare at me and watch me work with no expression. To hide my nervousness, I pretended I was busier than I was.

Soon, it was time for my 30-minute break at 7. It was Bambi who took my place. She wore an extraordinary cover-up to hide her skimpy costume and make her look more businesslike. As I turned to leave, I noticed Johnny eying her with a lascivious smile. I wondered whether Bambi felt the same way toward him or if he would cause her trouble.

With eyes glued to the floor, I went through the bar area into Romano's kitchen. When he saw me, he said, "Hi there, Rosebud! What can I do for you?"

"I was wondering if you could make me a sandwich for my dinner break. Cindy told me we could ask if you're not too busy …."

"For you, Rosebud, anything. Sit right here at the end of the prep table. I'll fix you something nice. Don't go to the break room where the rest of the girls are. You come here with me." He added protectively, "You can come here for all your breaks."

I breathed a sigh of relief. I felt comfortable and safe with Romano. However, I'd have to make time for the other girls if I were to learn anything about what was happening in this place. "Thanks so much, Romano! I will when I can."

"Now, how about a tuna sandwich topped with Greek olives and roasted pine nuts on dark rye?"

Just the thought of it made my mouth water. We chatted as he fixed the sandwich. Then Romano was the only one who talked because I was too busy filling my mouth with his wonderful concoction. Just like that, 30 minutes were up, and it was time for me to return to my spot. Romano and I air-kissed, and he whispered, "Remember, my little flower, you come *here* for your breaks."

I could not have known then how much of a blessing it would be to have Romano in my life or to what extent he would go to save my life in the future. Now, I was grateful to have the opportunity to become friends, for he was someone I intuitively knew I could trust.

As I entered the bar area, I was surprised to see Mike, dressed in a suit, with another man. They were at one of the café tables having a drink. Mike called me over. Reluctantly, I went. "Hi, there! I want you to meet Thomas."

Thomas looked and acted like he already had too much to drink. "Hi there, Linda!" he said with a wink.

Mike was watching me with a smile as I realized who this gentleman was—one of their employees. I shook hands with Thomas and corrected my name so it would seem natural to anyone nearby. I said my goodbyes crisply, then I hurried back to my position, feeling protected and safe with Mike, Thomas, and Romano surrounding me.

Shortly after, Mike came to the front desk to say goodbye. He gave me a peck on the cheek, saying, "Heading home to feed Sweet Pea. I bet she's wondering where we are. We'll be back at 10 to pick you up."

That was almost too much for me. I was beginning to feel way too comfortable having Mike around, and I needed to remember he was only acting a part, right? At least, I hoped so, for I had no intention of getting involved with any man.

CHAPTER 27

A s good as his word, Mike appeared with Sweet Pea at ten o'clock sharp. Cindy and I were talking together when he came through the door. "Hi there, handsome," she called out, "here to pick up your girlfriend, I see."

"Yup," was all Mike said.

Cindy and I looked at each other and laughed. Men! Sometimes you couldn't get them to say a thing. Sometimes it was best they didn't!

"I'll be right there, Mike," I said. "I have to get my purse."

"No problem," he responded.

As I passed the kitchen, I blew Romano a kiss and kept going. No time to chat. It looked as if his kitchen staff was closing up for the night. I'd heard the dinner hour was from 4:00 to 10:00 p.m., so I wasn't surprised. Just as I

181

turned to go down the hallway leading to the break room, I saw Johnny was coming from one of the closed-off offices where we weren't allowed. He looked sullen and didn't seem to notice me. His elbow caught me, forcing both of us to pause. He turned to me and barked, "Watch where you're going!"

I was annoyed and tired enough to say, "I think you'd better watch where you're going too."

He considered me then. "Really?"

I stood my ground and answered, "Yes."

Instead of being upset with me, he just gave a harsh laugh. I continued on my way before either of us could say any more.

As I came back through the bar area, I could see Johnny speaking to an older gentleman across the way. Both were watching me. I thought the other man might be David Masterly, who was in charge of the girls who danced there. If so, I understood that he also would be my boss. I would have to check with Brian to have him describe what David looked like. I arrived at my desk to find Mike laughing heartily with Cindy about something. As soon as he saw me, he stopped and came toward me. "Ready?"

"What was that all about?" I whispered.

"Nothing. Just schmoozing."

We left Cindy waving after us. With a sigh of relief, I climbed into the car to be greeted by Sweet Pea.

"Tired?" asked Mike.

"Not really," I answered.

"Good, because Brian and Thomas are meeting with us tonight. They should be at the house already."

They were pulling up in Brian's sports car when we arrived at my house. The car was easy to recognize with its brilliant red color. No incognito there, I thought. Once released, Sweet Pea raced to his car, and he greeted her enthusiastically. He began playing with her, and I assumed he'd pick her up and carry her inside when they finished.

I went in ahead of them. A few minutes later, Brian entered, and knowing what he'd want, I called out to him, "It's already on."

"A good woman, for sure, to know coffee is in order," he said enthusiastically.

As I rolled my eyes, the other two men looked at us with amusement, but neither said a word. I took orders for coffee before they went into the living room. I felt a swirl of air surround me and was happy to know Gram was there. I had missed her. She hadn't been around for a while. "I can feel your smile, Gram," I whispered.

"Yes, you can, Rosie girl. I love seeing you surrounded by handsome men helping to keep you safe."

"Don't even go there, Gram. I'm not interested in any of them. I have too much to do."

"Remember to keep your eyes open, for things aren't what they seem. Goodbye, my darling Sunshine." Off she went, sending me red roses for love.

I thought about what she'd said and remembered it was the same warning she had given me earlier—things aren't what they seem. I would keep that in mind.

As we sat around, Thomas began listing some Purple Passion Lounge players and their backgrounds. "We know Tony Angelo manages the club and is considered a part owner. But he doesn't own it; his uncle does. His uncle isn't well and has left it to Tony to manage. As much as we have looked into their backgrounds, there are only minor issues with the law."

"What about Sally?" I asked. "She was related to Tony, wasn't she?"

"Yes. She was his cousin, one of his uncle's daughters. Tony's mother and Sally's father were sister and brother," answered Mike.

"So, do we know why Sally was killed? Or by whom?" I asked.

Brian answered. "All we know is that those in charge felt she had betrayed them. We think it may be related to the codes you gave me."

I felt shivers all along my body. The codes had to be the answer to it all. Would it have made a difference if I had told Sally about the money? No, that wouldn't have helped her because I didn't know the codes existed then. Yet, I knew they held the answer. "What did you find out about the codes?" I asked.

"Nothing much," responded Thomas. "Yes, they're in anagram form with numbers, so it looks as if they're clients' names, with the number standing for what could be various sexual acts performed, according to the information you gave Brian. We'll be looking further into it."

Brian broke in. "Right now, we're more interested in how they get and distribute the drugs. That is where you come in, Rosie. Over the next several days, I will have one or possibly two men come to the lounge as clients, and they'll request recreational drugs before paying the entrance fee. You will pass on their requests to the higher-ups to see what you should tell them. Let's see what they have to offer."

I interrupted. "I think there must be drugs for sale there already because yesterday I walked by one of the lounge areas, and I could see through the curtains. It looked like someone was sniffing something, but I just kept walking," I shivered.

"What we think is happening is that some guys there for drugs walk out of the Purple Passion with bags of cocaine tied around their waists or ankles. Have you noticed guests coming in or out with large, baggy jackets or pants?"

"Yes, I have. I thought they were just sloppy, that's all."

"Well, now you know," concluded Brian.

"What we want you to do," he continued, "is copy down any information about them—name if you can get it, credit card info, and the like. We haven't been able to have someone like you inside there before without blowing our cover. We must remind ourselves not to spend so much time there that we draw attention to ourselves."

"Well, it's too bad you must cut your time short there," I said sarcastically.

The men chuckled, and the tension that had been swirling around dispersed. Then Thomas got up and looked at Brian. "That's it for now, right, Brian? Mike?"

"Sure thing," Brian answered as he got up and grabbed two of the empty coffee mugs. He tipped his head, motioning me to follow him back into the kitchen.

"How are things, Rosie girl? Are you all right with everything?"

"Sure. No problem."

"Are you and Mike getting along okay?"

I could feel my face turning red. "Yeah, fine. Why?"

"I want to make sure everything is fine between the two of you," he said before turning around and calling to Thomas that he was ready to go.

This time, while we were saying goodbye at the door, Brian hugged me and looked surprised. But he was probably no more astonished than I was. Mike and I stood together at the door watching the others leave. I was holding Sweet

Pea so she wouldn't run outside. Mike turned to me. "That was interesting, wasn't it?"

I could only nod, for what could I say? Brian was an enigma, hard to figure out at times.

CHAPTER 28

T he next day at work, I was left entirely alone — as if I'd been there forever. My job was not that hard, but even so … Johnny also took breaks away from the front area at the beginning of my shift before it got too busy to do so. I felt it was so he could watch Bambi performing inside the bar area. That allowed me to check out the lounging areas bordering the hallway leading into the bar. Nothing. All were empty. Perhaps there'd be something later when business picked up.

I knew I had been given the slower shift, which I was happy about. If I had to take the 10 p.m. to 4 a.m. shift, it'd be an even bigger adjustment for me. Sweet Pea was out of balance as it was. She's no different than me; we like to stick to a more "regular" daytime schedule. Thank God for Mike, who made sure she got fed on time. However, that couldn't last forever. Mike had other fish to fry.

David Masterly showed up just before my break. He must have come from the back, for I hadn't seen him arrive through the front. He was a man in his 50s, the same as his wife, Mama. The comparison between the two was astonishing, and it was hard to imagine them together. Where Mama was big and fat, David was thin and dwindling, if possible, for he was emaciated as it was. He looked like death warmed over. All around him was a heavy, dark energy filled with sadness that kept him bowed a bit. His eyes were tormented. I thought of Melissa and wondered whether she was the cause of all his unhappiness. Or had it just being married to Mama done that to him?

When David introduced himself to me, he didn't look me directly in the eye. It was as if he were avoiding any intimacy with me. "Rosalie, welcome to the Purple Passion Lounge. I'm David Masterly, your boss. You can talk to Mama or get one of the girls to find me if you need anything. Is everything okay so far?"

I grabbed his hand to shake it. He immediately pulled it away, but not before I connected with his energy and intuitively saw him and Mama arguing. A child was in the background, and I wondered who she was and what that was all about. I didn't feel safe with David despite the girls having said he was the one who protected them. But again, that was before Melissa's death. Was it different now? It didn't look as if he had the energy to protect anyone.

David left, and Bambi again relieved me for my break. She was wearing her special robe, which covered most of her body. I watched her stuff some bills into the pockets of her robe before she looked in my direction.

"Hey, Bambi, how's it going?

"Okay, girl. How about you?"

"David Masterly came by to say hello. What's his story?"

"He's a really good guy, or he certainly was before one of the girls here left and went on to other things."

"Are you talking about Melissa?"

"Yeah. How'd you know?"

"Word gets around. What happened?"

"We all knew David was sweet on Melissa. Mama was furious about it and caused her trouble any way she could. Finally, Melissa left and began working at PUP. The word is that David bought her the car needed for the job. That's all I know."

As Bambi finished telling me about David, Johnny came tearing around the corner. "Hey, you, stop your yapping and take your break now. Bambi's on a schedule and can't be here waiting on you to come back."

"Now, Johnny," interposed Bambi. "Let her be. It's my fault."

He seemed to ease his entire stance and said in a lighter tone, "Make sure you're back here on time."

I ran down the hallway. As I passed the lounging areas, I could barely make out a few people behind the drapes of one space. I hurried along to Romano's kitchen, and he was there waiting for me with a big smile. I loved that man, for he provided a haven to restore myself.

"I have something special waiting for you, my little Rosebud."

"Yummm. What is it?"

"One of my concoctions—a chicken casserole with a combination of cheeses, yellow peppers, lemon, garlic, and herbs."

"Oh, my God, Romano, you're the best!"

It was as good as promised. Romano loved to watch me eat because I made the appropriate sounds to express my pleasure. All too soon, my time was up. We air-kissed, and I went back down the hallway to my desk.

As I passed one lounge, I could see the people inside were readying themselves to leave. I noticed several of the men wearing baggy jackets. I raced back to my area, hoping they'd need to charge something and I'd be able to get their information. Bambi left, and I waited and waited. No one looking like either of the men I'd seen earlier came my way. Instead, just a few guys needed PUP transportation, but none with baggy jackets or pants.

I was startled by the noise a group of men made when they burst through the doors. Some of them wore oversized jackets and were a bit scary-looking. Fortunately, Johnny was there to guide them to my desk so they could pay their entrance fees. I was disappointed that only one had used a credit card while the rest paid cash.

Mama had me use a particular iPad that let me use Square to swipe the customer's credit card. I could send a receipt to the customer's email if they wanted, though I was told no one ever did. If that were the case, would it be possible to have the receipt sent to my email without anyone knowing about it? What about Square itself? Was there a way to look into the account and see where the money was deposited? Could I print out a list of customers who had used their credit cards? I would have to look into that or ask the guys about it.

The rest of the shift went along without anything useful happening. Cindy came early to relieve me so we could chat. I wondered if she did so because that might allow her to connect with Mike. Was I a bit jealous?

"Hey there, Rosebud! How's it going?" she asked with a twinkle in her eye. "Pretty boring at the desk, isn't it?"

"You've got that right. The only real interesting thing was meeting David Masterly. What's up with him?"

"He's all right. Can't say that about his wife, though. Mama is a piece of work and doesn't let him get away with a thing. She's on him like a rooster on a June bug. They don't even look like they belong together, right?"

I wanted to learn more about David, Melissa, and perhaps Sally. "I heard he was sweet on Melissa and Sally."

"Oh, no, not Sally. You know about Sally, right? Sally was Tony's cousin. Sally and David were strictly business. David cared about Melissa, though. He said she reminded him of his sister, who had died at about the same age as Melissa." Cindy paused. "Too bad what happened …."

"What happened?"

"Well, Melissa got in trouble with the bosses, so she left to work for PUP. We all knew that it was David who had bought her the car. But we were glad for her, you know? A new start and everything. It was Mama who was furious she left. One of the girls overheard her screaming at David something about 'You couldn't leave things alone, could you?' and some other stuff. Anyhow, after a couple of weeks went by, she was killed. You know about that, right?"

"Not that much, really. Who killed her?" I asked, playing dumb.

"The only thing I know is it had to be someone who had connections here because …."

Just then, Mike and Brian walked through the door together. Cindy hurriedly whispered, "It's the only thing that makes sense. Just be careful." She turned and gave her full attention to Mike. "Hi there, handsome. We know who you are here for, right, Rosebud?"

I'm sure I would have won the prize for the funniest home video if I could've snapped a video of Brian's face when he heard Cindy call me Rosebud. It looked as if he wasn't sure he'd heard it right, but then his cheeks turned pink from trying not to laugh. Brian turned his face away and started coughing. I'm sure he thought doing so would mask his laughter, which was not the case. Cindy and Mike tried not to laugh as they watched Brian and realized what had happened. I held my head high and said in a very professional voice, "Don't even think of saying a word, Cowboy. I'll be back as soon as I grab my purse."

All three faces turned to me, but no one uttered a sound. As I began my walk in silence down the hallway toward the break room, I heard laughter from the front area. As I passed the kitchen, I heard Romano shouting at someone. "This is my kitchen, and nothing or no one enters here unless invited, and you are not! My kitchen, my rules. Now get out! I'll quit before I allow anyone to tell me how to run my kitchen."

"Now calm down, Romano! No one wants you to leave. You are the chef supreme, and you know that. Let's pretend this never happened, okay?"

When I peeked in, I was surprised to see Tony Angelo and Mama standing there. I couldn't begin to imagine what the fuss was about. Perhaps Romano would share that with me tomorrow during my break time. I'd already decided to continue sitting with Romano for my dinner break. I would come into work at least a half hour early before my shift began so I could see what, if anything, I could pick up from the girls as they got ready for their shifts.

When I returned to the front desk, Brian and Mike laughed with Cindy, who was enjoying herself and entertaining the guys. She looked happy and gave me a big smile as I came forward. "They're all yours, Rosebud."

Both guys looked a bit embarrassed as Mike said, "Not so fast, Cindy." He winked at me and said, "Cindy talked us into staying for a bit. Here are the car keys for you. Brian will drop me off at the house later. I won't be too late, I promise."

What could I say? Indeed, not anything I was thinking. I took the car keys from Mike, feeling like the dutiful little woman ready to do whatever her man wanted. It certainly didn't feel good, despite knowing they were just doing their job. Mike bent to kiss me and whispered into my ear, "I promise I'll be good." I thought whatever that meant, trying to pretend I was not the least bit interested in anything he did.

Brian watched the interaction between Mike and me with a tight expression. What's wrong with him? I thought. It's only play-acting. I said my goodbyes, and off I went. When I gave my keys to the valet so he could pull my car up, I was surprised to find Johnny at my elbow. He didn't look happy, but then again, he never did. So I was surprised to hear him say in a professional voice, "Have a good night."

I turned to him and looked at him curiously. "Thanks, Johnny."

"Bambi says you're okay," he said as if that explained everything. Seemingly, what was good enough for Bambi was good enough for him. I'd have to remember that.

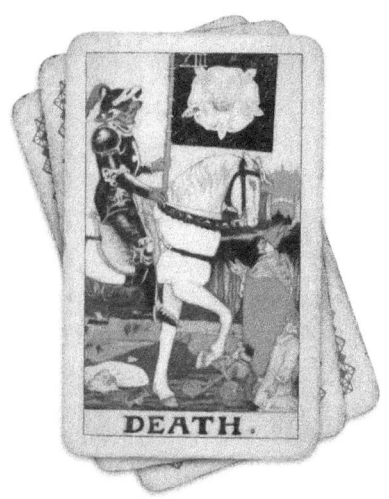

CHAPTER 29

S ince Mike had moved in, instead of lazing in the covers as usual in the morning, Sweet Pea was now the first to pop out of bed. She ran downstairs, with her little paws making their unique music on the wooden stairs, to be greeted by Mike, who fussed over her and tended to her needs. I didn't know when Mike slept, for no matter what time I woke up, I could hear him in the kitchen, and I smelled coffee brewing.

I got up and dressed in one of the outfits Louie had chosen for me. I was pleased with it. So was Mike, for as I came down the stairs, he looked me over and smiled. "You look gorgeous, Rosie."

It was interesting that Mike never called me Rosie girl as Brian sometimes did. Instead, it was simply Rosie. I could feel my cheeks turn pink with pleasure but tried to brush it off. "How was last night? I never even heard you come in."

"Slept on the couch so I wouldn't disturb you."

"That was nice of you. I slept well for a change."

Mike ran his hand through his messy hair and said, "Coffee's ready, and Sweet Pea's been out. I'm going to hop in the shower and get cleaned up."

"Okay. So you know, I want to go to work early today to see whether I can pick up any tidbits from the girls."

"Sounds good to me!"

Suddenly, the doorbell rang. I was surprised because I hadn't expected anyone. Sweet Pea went crazy with excitement. I looked at Mike, and he shrugged his shoulder and said, "It's probably Brian."

I answered the door, and as soon as Mike saw Brian, he gave him a wave and climbed the stairs, leaving me to entertain Brian.

"Good morning! How about a cup of coffee?"

"Yes, please." He looked me up and down and said, "You look nice."

As silly as it was, it irritated me that he couldn't be more like Mike and say I looked beautiful. His former phrase, "pretty enough," loomed before me. I studied him silently and noted he looked tired and a bit rumpled. I turned to go into the kitchen, and Brian followed on my heels, holding Sweet Pea in his arms.

"So, how was last night? Did you learn anything?"

"There's a lot of shit going on there, that's for sure."

"What do you mean?"

"Things aren't what they seem . . . I know it."

I shivered, for that was precisely what my grandmother had said to me. It was odd how often he used the same names and terms as she did. Is she and Brian connected somehow?

"What do you think is going on?" I asked.

"I think something big is going down in the next few days. I can feel it in my bones." He paused, "This might mean that Mike won't be able to be here every night."

He carefully watched me, and I tried not to show any reaction. I felt let down in a way that left me wondering about my attachment to Mike. Brian sensed it, too, for he quickly added, "I certainly won't leave you alone, though. I'll have surveillance here at the house."

"For heaven's sake," I snapped, "I'm perfectly capable of taking care of myself."

"That's not the issue, and you know it. Everyone knows you don't like to have to depend on anyone else. But you're in a vulnerable position right now, and I want you safe."

I looked at him but could not say what was on my mind. I realized how much these two men in my life were coming to mean to me. As much as Brian wanted me safe, I wanted the same for him and Mike. That old expression came to mind … "What a tangled web we weave when first we practice to deceive." I don't know why it was so difficult to be straightforward with Brian about anything, but there it was.

"Here's what I want you to do today if it pleases the lady," he said playfully. I knew he hated me for snapping at him, something I seemed to do too often. "I would like you to scout around a bit more to see if you notice any extra activity. Mike and I sensed more movement last night than ever."

"What kind of activity?"

"People were scurrying around or whispering among the bosses. Past the men's restroom, we heard doors opening and slamming shut like someone was in a hurry, that type of thing. That's the area where the offices are, right?"

"Yes, and those are off-limits to us girls. But I'll see what I can find out."

"Good! We're doubling the number of men on the premises for the next few days, so you'll never be alone."

"How will I recognize them?"

"If you go through the bar, you'll know who they are. They'll be more interested in drinking than gawking at the girls like other men."

I couldn't help asking, "Is that what you do there too?"

Maddeningly, Brian smiled and never answered, knowing that would annoy me.

Mike, all cleaned up and looking good, joined us. He looked from one to the other, sensing a bit of a conflict. Curious, he asked, "So what have you two been discussing?

"Just catching her up on what we experienced last night and telling her we expect something to go down soon. Also, to keep her eyes and ears open," he added.

Mike looked at me and asked, "Did Brian tell you I won't be here tonight? I'll leave the car keys with you so you can drive to work and home later. Once your shift ends, you need to come straight home, though, understand?"

Mike was beginning to sound like a worried father again, and I teased him by saying, "Yes, Dad."

That annoyed him, especially since he was just a few years older than me, but he held back a reply.

Brian reminded me, "Keep your cell phone with you at all times, and use it if you need to get ahold of me."

Luckily, I wore flowing black pants with deep pockets, so that wouldn't be a problem. I had already programmed my voice command for Brian's and Mike's telephone numbers, which would speed things up if I needed to call either one.

I left them in the kitchen sitting at the table, setting up the schedule for their men as I wandered into my office. I had taken my tarot cards from the living room, where I usually kept them, and put them in the office. As I reached for them, the bag holding them slipped and fell—almost as though pushed. Down they went, and one card popped out. I picked it up to see that it was the Death card. So the end was getting close, I thought with a thumping heart. I hoped with all my heart that the Death card wasn't meant for Brian, Mike, me—or anyone else I cared about.

It was odd, too, that I had pushed away much of my intuition while taking part in this undercover scheme at the Purple Passion Lounge. I had wanted to play it straight, but what was the sense in that? We all needed to do what we could so fewer people got hurt.

Thanks to my lawyer and best friend, Susannah, I'd gotten all my paperwork in order in case anything happened to me. I even had to sign a specific document the state of Nevada requires so that Sweet Pea wouldn't go directly to the pound when I died. My neighbor had accepted the responsibility to remove her from my house until Nancy, one of my other close friends, could claim her.

My heart was heavy as I realized how vulnerable we all were. Mike handed me the car keys, and the guys left to do their own thing. I was left there watching the two of them disappear through the door, and I wondered what this day would have in store for all of us.

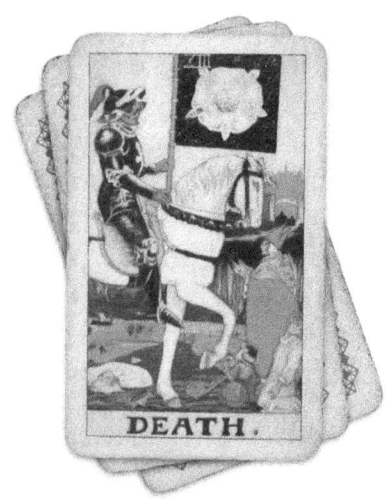

CHAPTER 30

Before long, it was time for me to go to work. I was curious to see what I'd discover. Once I arrived, it was too early for the valet, so I parked the car myself and walked to the front. I had to ring the buzzer for someone to let me in, and as I waited, a young girl I had never seen before came up next to me. "I'm so excited. It's my first day at work here!" As she looked me over, she asked curiously, "What type of dancing do you do?"

I laughed and said, "Not much of anything. I'm Rosalie. I'm the 'welcome girl' at the front desk."

She put her hand out to shake mine and said, "I'm Shirley. Nice to meet you."

As she touched my hand, I envisioned her lying on the floor with blood pooling around her and someone standing over her with a gun. I felt faint and stumbled back, letting

Shirley be the first through the door as Johnny stood there. He gave me a funny look and said, "Are you all right?"

"I'm okay, thanks. How are you, Johnny?"

"C'mon in," he mumbled, not answering me.

I had to be careful not to let my intuition pick up all I was sensing around me, or I would go crazy. I returned to the employee lounge and put my purse into my locker before fixing myself a cup of coffee. Then I sat at the large table for us girls to use. I watched Shirley bounce around, talking with three other young dancers who had come into the break room. "I'm so excited! So tell me, do the men give big tips?"

"It depends on what you do for them," remarked one of the other girls. "You're new at this, right?"

"Yes, my boyfriend would kill me if he knew what I was doing. I want to make enough money so that we can get married. That's why I'm here."

"Shirley, maybe you should do something else to earn enough money to get married, maybe something with better hours." From what she had said about the boyfriend, it made sense that he was probably the one with the gun in my vision. Even though I couldn't be sure of the outcome of any image I had, I couldn't help myself and interfered.

"Like what?"

"You could waitress. You can earn big tips, and it would be safer too. Have you ever waitressed before?"

"No, and I've already decided this is what I want to do," she answered emphatically.

The other girls looked at me, obviously curious about my suggestion she should do something other than dance there. Shirley turned back to them and asked, "It's fun, right?"

Now all three of the girls smiled and talked all at once. "That depends … " one of them said.

Another added, "Maybe for the first few days. Then it becomes work, like anything else."

The third one looked at the other two and said, "The newbies always think it is more glamorous than it is, don't they?" The three of them nodded their heads in agreement.

The first girl warned Shirley, "Stay clear of Mama. She can be a b-i-t-c-h if you know what I mean."

I watched them, knowing each had her own journey. I could only offer up a suggestion to do something else; the rest was up to them. I knew my time was up, and I'd better hurry to the front. I said goodbye to the girls, wishing them well. "Have a good day."

I heard one of them ask, "Who was that?"

The response I heard came from Shirley. "She's the older lady who works at the front desk. I forget her name."

I had to smile. Older lady at 32? Oh, my. I passed Romano's kitchen and blew him a kiss. As I turned the corner to the front, I was glad to see Cindy there. She pulled at my heartstrings in ways I couldn't explain. Cindy smiled at me, and I thought, What was she doing working here anyway? She wasn't supposed to be scheduled if I was here.

"Hey, Rosebud, how goes it?" Cindy asked.

"So far, so good." I liked Cindy, for she was older than many girls and didn't act like them either. She didn't seem to lose herself in the business as they did. She had taken over David Masterly's scheduling and other smaller tasks. I was curious about her. "How long have you been working here, Cindy?"

"Probably longer than is good for me. Why?"

"I don't know. I can picture you in a more corporate setting, that's all. We knew our jobs here didn't suit us, making us laugh together. "Nothing against here, of course," I added.

Then she became serious. "Well, I tried that once. It was all over as soon as word about what I had done before got out. Every guy in the company harassed me, trying to get into my pants. You know how that goes, right?"

I paused, somewhat curious about why she thought that had happened to me—men wanting to get into my pants. Perhaps. But I've always been accused of ignoring any attention any man gave me. "I get it," was all I answered.

Cindy was bright and had street smarts and a lot going for her. I could see her working for Brian or Mike undercover, where her background could be an asset. Perhaps that was an idea to run by Brian or Mike? She'd be great.

Cindy leaned toward me and whispered, "I don't know what's happening, but all the bigwigs are jumpy. I overheard them talking about special guests coming in a day or two. I don't know what that means. I tried asking David about it, and his face fell. He immediately turned his back on me and walked out of the office. Just want to warn you, that's all. Pretend you know nothing, all right?"

I had to smile, for that would be easy for me to do because I had no clue what was going on. Cindy left, and I was somewhat surprised to find myself pretty busy until Bambi came to relieve me. I asked her, "What's going on here? I've never seen it this way!"

"I don't really know. Mama has something planned, though. She's rattled."

"Oh, well. I guess we'll find out soon enough. I'll be back in thirty," I said.

I was happy to take my break and head to the kitchen to see Romano. I couldn't wait to see what he had prepared for me.

"Ah, my little Rosebud. How are you?"

We air-kissed, and he still seemed upset. "Are you okay?" I asked him. "You seem upset."

He practically hissed at me, "The owners here want to take over my kitchen tomorrow night. They have something special planned. They even want me to close down the kitchen for the entire night. I absolutely refuse to have anyone but me in my kitchen, or they can find someone else for this job!"

"Whoa, you're really angry! So what are you going to do?"

Romano leaned in closer and whispered, "I'll be cooking for a buffet they will hold in the pool area. I'm not supposed to say anything to anybody about this, so it's between us, okay?"

"No problem. Mum's the word." My mind began whirling around what had been said. I would have to reach Brian and pass on this information.

Romano seemed relieved to spout off about his anger, and within a blink of an eye, he put on his usually happy face and said, "My darling Rosebud, I have fixed a surprise for you."

I adored surprises and couldn't wait to see what he had concocted for me. "So tell me, what is it?"

"Hungarian chicken paprika, an old recipe that will make you weep. Wait right here, and I'll bring it over."

It was delicious, with its creamy sauce and smooth taste served over rice with a fresh green salad. It was worth every ounce I knew I would gain from eating it. My, that man sure knew how to cook.

205

I looked at the clock and knew that if I hurried, I would have enough time to go to the employee lounge to reapply my lipstick. I air-kissed Romano and gave him a little hug, which he returned. I raced down the hallway. When I opened the door to the lounge, I didn't see anyone inside, although I had the eerie sense that someone was in the room with me. I went to my locker and nearly fainted when someone tapped my shoulder. I turned around, and there was a child about ten years old. She whispered something to me in a language I didn't quite understand. The only word I could make out was "mama." I felt at a loss when I realized she was trying to get my help, but I couldn't understand what she wanted.

"Are you looking for your mother?"

When she heard the word mother, she nodded her head. "Does she work here?" I asked.

Just then, the door opened, and Johnny stood there. "I think she's looking for her mother," I said.

"What else did she say?" he demanded.

"I don't know. I can't understand what she's saying because I don't know her language."

"I'll take it from here," he ordered. "Go! You're late to relieve Bambi."

I ran out without applying any lipstick. What was that all about? I wondered.

Bambi was generous as always in not being upset that I was late to relieve her. Nothing seemed to bother her. Unfairly, I wondered if she was on any drugs.

Soon, I was surprised to see Thomas arrive, and, true to his word, he asked me if drugs were available for purchase. "I don't know about that, sir," I played along.

"I was told this was the place to come. I want to see the manager!" he demanded. Johnny must be tending to the girls, I thought, for he was not in the front as usual. Another security guard must have heard Thomas's loud voice, for he stepped from the smaller hall into the reception area and came to where we were standing.

"What's going on?" he asked.

"This gentleman is asking about drugs, and I don't have the answer. He's demanding to see the manager," I responded.

"Let me get Tony," said the guard. "Sir, stay right where you are, hear?"

Thomas nodded in agreement and remained where he was, leaning on my desk. "Nice job," he whispered.

"I'll get him on my radio," the security guard advised before he turned away to get some privacy. We could still hear him talking to Tony.

Tony came rushing out, and seeing me there, he looked perplexed. Tony had made no effort to introduce himself to me and looked like he expected someone else to be at the desk. "It's all right ..." He couldn't say my name because he didn't know it.

Thomas stepped in to ease the awkwardness. "Tony? I've been told I can purchase what I need here, if you know what I mean," he said, giving Tony a wink, "as long as I'm with one of the girls. Is that right?"

I watched Tony smoothly push Thomas into the hallway leading to the bar area. I noticed that Thomas was wearing a baggy jacket. Guess I'd find out later if he succeeded in getting drugs.

It was nearly time for Cindy to relieve me when Brian and Mike arrived. Johnny was back on duty in the front area and eyed them as they greeted me. "Hi, Sunshine!" said Brian. I smiled, glad to see him. With Johnny watching our every move, Mike stepped forward as my boyfriend to welcome me with a kiss. I kissed him back, pleased to be doing more than acting our parts, and I saw Brian scowling as we pulled apart.

Cindy came round the corner and brightened when she saw Mike standing there. "Hi, handsome."

He smiled at her and said, "How's it going, Sweet Thing?"

I looked at Mike. I said nothing, for I hadn't realized he knew her nickname. He looked at me, and his cheeks reddened. He said, "If it's okay with you, I'm going to stay and have a drink with Brian. He's falling for that cute little redhead and can't take his eyes off her," he teased.

Bambi? Brian whipped around to look at Mike at the same time Johnny did. Both wore a surprised look, and murderous looks soon followed. Mike didn't realize he was setting Brian up for real trouble from Johnny if he made the tiniest move on Bambi, and Brian didn't like to be played by anyone, much less Mike.

Cindy collected their money. I waited for them so we could walk down the hall together toward the bar area. As we rounded the corner from Johnny's view, I pulled on Brian's sleeve and whispered what I had learned from Romano about tomorrow night's big event. I told him that Thomas was here somewhere too.

"Nice work, Rosie!" he said, patting my shoulder in appreciation. "Go home now. No worries. I've got surveillance watching the house." He paused a moment before adding, "I know. You don't need my help," looking a bit peeved by the look I gave him.

"Actually, I'm glad you arranged that," I said, surprising him. He looked at me in confusion, then pleasure, for having said something right for a change. He shook his head back and forth a few times. "See you later."

I walked through the bar and headed down the hallway to the employee lounge. Before I got there, I heard loud noises from the pool area and went to see what was happening. I peeked through the door, which was propped open, and saw several men lining up chairs in two rows facing a podium. That's interesting, I thought. I wonder who will be giving a speech—and on what subject? I heard footsteps coming down the hallway and quickly turned and raced back to stand by the entrance of the employee lounge as if I had just arrived. I wanted to see who was heading my way.

Mama came into view and was surprised to see me standing there. She looked at her watch, checked the time, and said dismissively, "Time for you to go home. See you tomorrow."

"Good night, Mama," was all I said.

Two dancers were sitting at the table drinking coffee in the employee lounge. Instead of getting my purse and heading straight home, I sat down with them to drink a glass of water, hoping I would overhear some gossip. Sure enough, I heard the first ask her friend, "What the heck is going on?"

The second one answered. "Who knows? Mum's the word. Mama is so uptight that she's about ready to explode."

"Oh, well. I'm sure we'll find out soon enough."

Both of the girls got up to leave. They smiled at me and said, "Have a good night," in unison. We all looked at each other and chuckled before going our way.

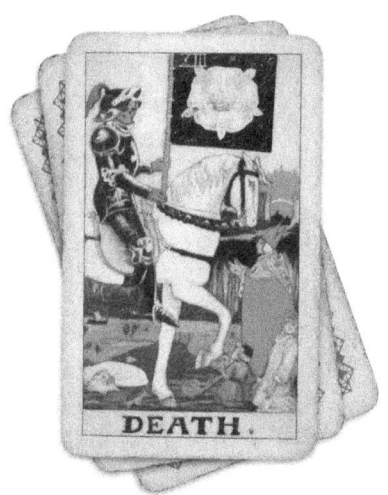

CHAPTER 31

W hen I got home, I could see Sweet Pea was upset. It was late, and although she had food set out for her, she had no interest in eating without an audience. I guess dogs feel the same way humans do about dining alone. I picked her up and carried her into the living room, holding her close and saying sweet things to her. Then I put on some music and poured myself a glass of wine, even though it was late. I sat at the kitchen table to watch Sweet Pea eat her dinner. Though tired and keyed up, I hoped to fall asleep and sleep soundly.

Instead, I tossed and turned all night and looked at the clock every hour or so. Part of me was waiting for Mike to come home so I would know all was okay. The last time I looked at the clock, it was 3:15. I must have fallen asleep after that, for it was Sweet Pea bouncing around on the bed that woke me up at 6:30. I couldn't hear Mike moving around or smell coffee brewing either, so I guessed he wasn't home.

I got up, put on my robe, and checked the guest room. It was empty. I went downstairs and began to brew a pot of coffee. Walking past my shiny stainless steel refrigerator, I saw my reflection, which wasn't good. It looked as if I had the most giant afro since Diana Ross. Hers looked good. Mine did not.

The doorbell rang, and Sweet Pea went crazy. I glanced through the peephole, and there was the Batman and Robin duo of Brian and Mike. Both looked as bad as I did. Even so, I wished I had, at the very least, brushed my teeth and put moisturizer on my face. I felt so unattractive that I was beginning to feel sorry for myself. I opened the door to let them in, and, as tired as they were, they brightened when they saw my hair. I watched them struggle to remain straight-faced. They didn't have to say a word, for it was written all over their faces. "C'mon in. Coffee's brewing," I said, ignoring the look they gave each other.

We sat at the kitchen table, drinking our coffee and reviewing what had happened. I was curious to find out about Thomas. "Did Thomas get his drugs?"

"Just some pot," answered Brian. "They vet people before supplying them the heavy stuff."

"Huh. I guess that's a smart thing for them to do. How did you make out with Bambi?"

Mike started to laugh, and Brian walloped him on the upper arm. "Ouch! Don't get mad at me! You should've known better than to step on any man's territory!"

I could see it. As handsome as Mike was, he didn't have the smooth moves of a man who had been around the ladies that much. I found that part of his charm. But if Brian showed even the slightest interest in Bambi, I knew Johnny would get back at him in some way. "What happened?" I asked.

"Brian tried to play up to Bambi a bit. After a while, I could tell Johnny was getting really pissed at us," answered Mike. "Then Johnny came to our table, dragging another young dancer behind him. He leaned down and whispered, 'This girl is more your speed, fellas.' She was new and didn't know what she was doing. It was embarrassing, and everyone was watching us. She was all over Brian and trying to do things that were ...."

"Oh, my God," I said. "That must have been Shirley!"

"Well, you can just imagine," Mike finished. Both men looked at each other and began to laugh at themselves.

I watched them, thinking boys will be boys. Men don't grow up, do they? Then I asked Brian, "What else did you find out?"

"You're right," Brian answered thoughtfully, "it appears something's going down tomorrow night. You could feel the excitement in the air."

"I think so, too," I said. "After leaving you two last night, I went into the pool area because I heard noises. It looked as if they were expecting quite a few people the way they are setting up and arranging everything."

Brian interrupted me. "Well, we'll be there at the Purple Passion tonight. Maybe we can get into whatever's going on. Can you see what you can do to make that happen, Rosie girl?"

"I'll try," I responded, wondering how to pull that off.

"Well," said Brian, looking at his watch as he drained the last of his coffee, "I'm going to report into the station, and then I'm going home to get a few hours of shut-eye before we regroup. How about you, Mike? Can you grab a few hours?"

"I'll head upstairs as soon as I finish my coffee. What time are we meeting?"

"I want us all to meet at 1 o'clock in Thomas's hotel room. Then I want to get to the lounge while Cindy is still there. Maybe she knows something she'd be willing to share with us. I'll leave that up to you, Mike, since she seems so interested in you," he teased.

"Right on," Mike responded.

I felt a pang of jealousy. Brian didn't need Mike or me at the lounge as long as Cindy was there. I scolded myself for thinking that nothing could happen without me. Does jealousy become a part of how girls change if men are in their lives? If so, I was no different. In addition, I needed to recognize that I wasn't dating Brian or Mike, nor were they "in my life" that way. Time to close the door on going down that path, I thought.

Brian left, and Mike went upstairs to shower and nap. I began to dust and vacuum, putting away a few things out of place. Whenever I'm upset, I clean. Afterward, I went into my office and finished up a column I was writing for *Women Living Well* about the energy of jealousy—something I was intimately familiar with at the moment. It turned out pretty well and helped give me a different perspective on my feelings. I'm just human, after all.

Mike was soon up and called to have one of the men in Brian's group pick him up at the house. He said he had work to do before meeting Brian at one o'clock. He kissed me lightly on the cheek, primarily by habit now, and headed out the door, much to Sweet Pea's dismay.

I was sleepy and knew I'd have time to nap before getting ready for work. Believing we might be right about it all going down tonight, I knew it would be a long night for all of us, and it would be a good idea to be well-rested.

I cuddled in bed with Sweet Pea beside me and immediately fell asleep. My dreams were wild and real. In one, my feet were as heavy as cement when I tried to run toward the outstretched hand of the young girl I had seen at the Purple Passion Lounge. I could hear a parade of feet racing behind me, running faster than I was. They were getting closer and closer. The girl kept hollering, "Help me! Help me, please!" I started to scream as I felt a hand grabbing me from behind. I abruptly woke up with Sweet Pea standing over me, wearing a worried expression and making small mewling sounds.

I sat up in bed, covered my eyes with my hands, and thought about the girl. I'd read enough to know how drug cartels get drugs into the United States. I'd heard of young girls wearing sanitary napkins filled with drugs. Another way was to have a mother with a child accompanying her carry stuffed toys—once a Mr. Potato Head—filled with powdered drugs. Was this girl being used like that?

I stood in the shower washing my hair, and as water poured down my body, I couldn't get the vision of my dream out of my head. I felt the girl had something to do with all that was happening at the lounge. I wasn't sure how it would all play out, but I guessed we'd find out soon enough, I thought with a twist of my heart. If I had to protect her, I had no doubt I'd do so.

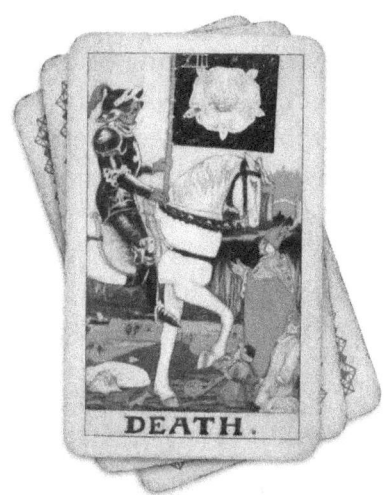

CHAPTER 32

I was almost late for work. I felt sluggish after my nap and couldn't decide what to wear. I pulled out another pair of flowing pants with deep pockets because I knew I needed to have my phone with me in case I had to contact Brian or Mike. The top I chose showed more cleavage and had more material flowing down, giving the outfit a casual but sensual look. Perfect.

When I arrived at the lounge, I was alert and ready for whatever the evening would bring. I was surprised to see Mama, not Cindy, at the front desk waiting for me. She was wearing makeup, which did nothing for her other than make her look clownish. She was a bit messy, and she seemed excited. "Oh, there you are!" she called out impatiently. "I need to talk to you. I have some important guests coming later, and I want to make sure you don't charge them the entrance fee."

"No problem, Mama. Do you have their names for me?"

"No names. They'll tell Johnny or you that they're here to see me. Johnny is the one who'll bring them to me. If anyone asks for me after Johnny has left with a guest, have him wait with you or Cindy until Johnny returns."

"Okay. I understand."

I must have had a curious look when I heard Cindy would be here with me. She added, "I want the two of you here at the front desk after your break. I trust that's not a problem."

I could feel my face brighten. "No problem, Mama."

"All right, then. See that you follow my orders."

She left me wondering what exactly was going on. I still had my purse with me, and when Johnny came into the front area, I asked him, "Would you mind watching the desk so I can put my purse in my locker?"

"Take your time," he said, unlike previous times when he ordered me to hurry. Yes, something was going on, all right.

"Thanks, Johnny."

As I cut through the bar, I saw Thomas sitting at one of the smaller café tables with one of the dancers. It looked like Thomas was drinking something bubbly, maybe even a Sprite or a 7up. It looked like the girl had been drinking something more potent, for she seemed to drape across the table as she reached for his hand. I ignored them, and I didn't see either Mike or Brian. I hurried along until I stopped by to say hello to Romano.

"My darling Rosebud!" he enthused as I passed his kitchen. I stopped, turned, and stepped into his kitchen. We air-kissed, and he looked pleased to see me.

He hugged me and whispered, "You are a breath of fresh air! Everyone is in such a dither around here; it's just been crazy!"

"What's going on?"

"Nothing good for sure. You can count on that."

"What do you mean?"

"If Mama puts on makeup, we're all in trouble," he responded with distaste.

"I saw the pool room yesterday; it looks like they will have a big meeting. Do you know what that's all about?"

"No, but all the food is ready for them—or will be in about an hour or two. I'm to begin serving at 9, and I have strict orders that I'm the only one allowed in the pool area. I must let my help go no later than 7:00 p.m. and serve the food myself. Can you imagine?" asked Romano voicing displeasure, which rose in pitch at the end of the sentence.

"Poor Romano. That's not right. You shouldn't have to be the one to serve."

"Ah, well. Life is not fair, my little flower."

"So I won't see you tonight then for my break. Well, good luck with …."

"Oh, no, my little Rosebud. You still come to me."

"Are you sure?"

"Yes, you can be the first to taste whatever you want from the buffet."

"Thank you, my dear friend."

Romano puffed up and generously said, "And you are mine."

I hurried down the hallway to the employee lounge. As I put my purse into my locker, I broke a nail. "Damn!" I said out loud. I pulled my purse back out of my locker, took out my special small, metal nail file kit, and slid it into the pocket that wasn't holding my phone. I'd fix it at my desk. Right now, I had to get back to Johnny ASAP.

I had just opened the door from the employee lounge into the hallway when I thought I heard someone crying. The sound came from one of the closed offices we weren't allowed to enter. I stood there for a few seconds, but I heard nothing more. It must be my imagination, I thought. Then the vision of the little girl in my dream floated before me, and I shivered. I stood there a few more seconds, but all was silent. I ran down the hall, past Romano's kitchen, into the bar area. I didn't bother looking for Brian or Mike.

When I arrived at the front desk, Johnny didn't seem upset I had taken so long. He said, "It's all yours," and walked away.

Time passed. It seemed to be the usual type of men coming in. Those who were obviously on vacation and wanted to experience what they thought Las Vegas was all about. And those more experienced guests who knew what they were getting into, and those men who were drunk and obnoxious, keeping both Johnny and the valet out front busy trying to keep things in order. In other words, there was nothing unusual.

I remembered the pool area had a separate entrance and wondered whether some guests would enter and leave there. It probably was too early to tell, as I didn't think the special guests would arrive until around eight or so if dinner would be served at nine.

Cindy showed up at seven o'clock sharp. I was glad to see her. I felt a little guilty for being jealous of her over Mike, for she was a great person. Cindy was also happy to see me, giving me a big hug. "Hey there, Rosebud! I'm glad we're together tonight!"

"Me, too. Do you know what is going on?"

She searched around to see where Johnny was. When she saw he was standing outside with the valet, she said in a low voice, "I wish I did. Ever since I returned to work here nine months ago, things have not been the same. We've had two deaths ..." and after seeing my face when she said deaths, she amended, "We've had two murders, and for what? Some of the girls are getting hooked on drugs now. That was never allowed before. That'd have never happened if Sophia were still alive."

Hearing Sophia's name spoken made my heart fall. "What was Sophia's role?"

"She had a tiny piece of the business, and her boss had the rest of their 60 percent ownership ...."

"How do you know all this?" I interrupted.

"I've taken over some of David's responsibilities. He is very careless about what he leaves around, so it's pretty easy for me to figure things out."

How Melissa could have gotten those pages with codes was making so much sense now. On a whim, I asked Cindy, "Did Melissa have a special nickname for David?"

Cindy chuckled. "David would die if he knew I had once heard them whispering together. She called him Big Boy, of all things!"

I felt lightheaded. Of course, it would've been David who had given Melissa the big diamond ring. And lord knows, all you had to do was look at him to know he's never gotten over her death.

"Big Boy" must undoubtedly refer to his anatomy. In a flash, I thought of Brian being teased by his friends calling him B.B. I could see that now. No wonder he turned red whenever they called him that.

I couldn't help myself. I began to laugh until tears rolled down my face. I was a mess, hiccupping and laughing at the same time. Cindy looked as if she didn't know whether to shake me or slap me. Finally, she just joined in the laughter. We hugged, held each other up, and continued laughing. We barely heard the gentleman in front of us clearing his throat. When we realized he was standing there, we immediately let go of each other and turned to him.

"I'm here to see Mama," he said in a clipped, hurried tone.

"I'll get Johnny," I said to Cindy, who nodded in agreement as she wiped her eyes on a tissue.

Johnny looked at me in a funny way, but he strode forward, shook the man's hand without saying a word to me, and led him to the back. Cindy and I looked at each other, wondering whether it was the same person we thought it was. "That was Roman Castille, wasn't it?" I asked.

"It sure was," answered Cindy.

"I wonder why a porn star would have anything to do with Mama."

"Beats me." Cindy looked at me and smiled. "Rosebud, you need to go and fix your makeup. Your mascara is all over your face."

"Oh, no! You've got to be kidding! I wondered why Johnny looked at me in a funny way. I'll hurry back."

"Take your time. Why don't you take your break as well? No need to hurry back; we're off our schedule anyhow."

"Thanks, Cindy. See you later!"

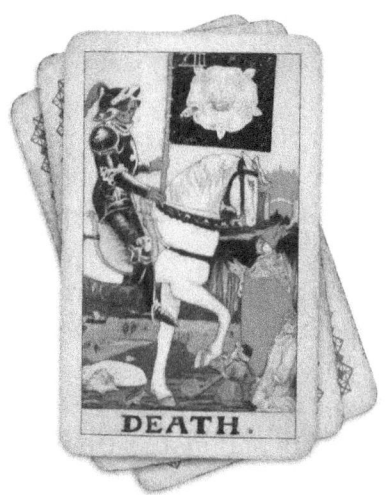

CHAPTER 33

I stepped into the women's restroom and threw water across my face to wash away the mascara that was indeed all over my face. That laughter with Cindy had done me good, and I looked happy despite what was happening around me. I washed my hands and headed to the employee lounge, where I could touch up my makeup and look half-decent again. As I reached the door to go inside, I again heard what sounded like someone crying.

I was determined to see who or what was making that noise this time. I went farther down the hallway past the first, then the second closed, off-limits office. It was at the third door that I heard scuffling sounds. I lightly tapped at the door and called, "Anyone there?"

I heard more furtive scrambling. "Please, is anyone there?"

I felt more than heard a person on the other side of the door. Then I could barely make out a whisper, "Help me, please."

I tried the handle of the door, but it was locked. I shook it a bit, hoping the lock wasn't seated. Nothing. I remembered the nail file was still in my pocket, so I took it out, put it into the lock, and wiggled it around, hoping I could unlock the door. In the distance, I heard someone determinedly coming down the hallway. Once whoever it was rounded the corner, the person would see me, and I would be in big trouble. I shook the door handle and twisted the nail file again. The lock opened just as the footsteps got closer. I went inside, quietly closed the door, and hoped no one would check this office.

I looked into the eyes of the girl I had seen yesterday and held my finger to my lips to signal her to be quiet. I waited until I heard the steps go further down toward the pool area before I turned around and searched the room. There were four young girls, all looking about 10 to 12 years old. Then it hit me. I knew exactly what was happening. There would not be a drug bust; this was all about human trafficking!

I felt sick remembering how the pool room was arranged. Were they really planning to auction these girls? It was set up that way. Oh, my God! I had to remain calm, and I had to get these girls out and keep them safe. How was I going to do that? I heard a cart coming down the hallway and knew it had to be Romano. I held my finger to my lips and told the girl, "Keep the others quiet."

As I turned to leave, the girl grabbed my arm and begged me with her eyes not to leave her there. I looked into her eyes and said, "I'll be right back, I promise. You have to trust me." She nodded her head, and I stepped outside just before Romano pushed his food cart my way. It was fancy, with a long white tablecloth covering it. I knew then I had found their means of escape.

"Ah, Rosebud, what are you doing here?"

"Romano, can I trust you?"

"With anything, my little flower! What's wrong?"

"You have to promise …."

"I'll do whatever you need. Just tell me what it is!"

I tugged his arm and pulled him into the room to face the four little girls, who stood huddled together, staring back at us. The two smallest ones had tear-stained faces, while the older two looked 90 years old because of the hopelessness in their eyes. It took Romano a few seconds to realize what was going on. "Oh, my God! What have we got here?"

"Little girls who will be sold unless we help them escape. Are you in or not?"

"What can I do?"

"Here's my plan," I said, "see whether you agree. Let's put this girl and one of the younger ones on the cart's bottom shelf, and you immediately go back to the kitchen as if you have forgotten something. I'll follow you and get them settled into the kitchen storage area. Then, on your way back from taking more food to the pool area, you'll stop by this door, settle the other two on the lower shelf, and return to the kitchen."

After I hurriedly explained what I wanted to do, Romano nodded in agreement. One of the two older girls spoke enough English to understand our plan. She explained that to the other three. They nodded their heads in agreement. "Okay, let's get started," I said.

I listened at the door and heard nothing, so I grabbed the two girls who would be transported first and got them underneath the cloth. Just as the last leg disappeared, we heard someone coming our way. Romano and I looked at each other in alarm and tried to remain calm. As we headed down the hall, I began chatting with Romano as if it were the most natural thing in the world. It was Johnny leading another special guest toward the pool room. "On your break, I see."

I smiled and said, "Yes, I am."

Johnny continued down the hallway. We hurried the cart along to the kitchen. Romano's other helpers had punched out for the night, thank God. We pushed the cart to the kitchen storage area and helped the girls out. Romano immediately returned to the pool area to pick up the other girls. I moved some boxes of paper towels, napkins, and other goods to create a hiding place. I gently positioned the two girls behind the boxes, placed my finger to my lips, so they knew to be quiet, and signaled them not to move.

I waited there in the kitchen area. The 15 minutes it took for Romano to return seemed like hours. As he entered the kitchen, his face was red, and he was sweating heavily. The second pair of girls got out of the cart, and we put them with the others, motioning for them to stay there and be quiet. Romano, true to who he was, gave each of them several cookies to eat and small bottles of water to drink.

We were lucky the storage area was a space behind the large walk-in refrigerator and freezer on the back wall, so you had to come in behind them. Unless you were standing right in front of it, you wouldn't even know the doorway to the storage area was there because the refrigerator and freezer blocked the entrance. Beside it was a door that opened to the outside. However, it was no use trying to escape there at this time. The girls wouldn't know where to go, and they would be picked off in a hurry by the extra security guards on duty tonight.

Right now, it was essential to keep the girls safe. To block off the girls' hiding place, Romano and I hoisted boxes in front of where they sat, so it looked like there was no empty space. Romano had had a delivery that morning, so we had enough boxes to pull it off.

We looked at each other, both in disarray by now, and smiled at our cleverness, but we both realized there was trouble ahead, and we'd have to face the music at some point. My break was over, and I wouldn't have time to eat. Romano also had to check the pool area and ensure everything was in order.

"My dear Romano, I don't know how to thank you for helping me. I hope I haven't gotten you into trouble that neither of us can escape."

"Not to worry, my little Rosebud. What you're doing is the right thing to do. We must find a way to get the girls out of here."

"I'll see what I can do," I promised. I was glad it was Cindy instead of Bambi out front, or Johnny would have sought me out long before this.

I slipped into my spot at the front desk, and Cindy looked concerned. "Are you okay? What's wrong?"

"I'm not feeling that great, but I'll be okay," I lied.

It was written all over her face that Cindy knew I wasn't telling the truth. I was worried to death about the girls, and I wondered how I was going to get them out without being caught.

"What's really going on?" Cindy asked me.

"Oh, Cindy, I ..."

We heard a screech from the back of the building; it was that loud. There was one loud, long wail, and then all went quiet. I said nothing to Cindy and waited to see what would happen next. Nothing. I saw the large advertising truck pull by the porte cochere through the one-way window as we stood together. Sally's picture was plastered on it as if she were still alive and available. I found that depressing. Then it hit me. Perhaps, it would be Sally who could help the girls escape.

"Cindy, what's that truck doing here?

"You mean the advertising truck? We own it; it's ours. Sometimes they keep it here overnight. That's probably what they're doing now."

That could work, I thought. All I needed were the keys to the truck. Then I could pull it up to the door in the kitchen, and because it was so big, it would block anyone from seeing us as we loaded the girls inside and took off with them.

"Cindy, I need your help. Can I trust you?" Cindy looked long and hard, deep into my eyes. My heart began to gallop, fearing that I had made a mistake by asking her.

"Tell me what's going on," she demanded.

I had to believe I hadn't read her wrong about her not being part of what was happening. I swallowed hard and quickly filled her in. I expected her to be surprised and alarmed by what she heard, but she took it all in stride.

"Stay right here. I'll get the keys," Cindy said.

My body felt like putty, and I could hardly stand up. I had been so tense while waiting for Cindy's answer that my body felt drained of all strength. I tried to regroup, but the minutes waiting for Cindy to return were painfully long and filled with anxiety. When she returned, she was not alone. Johnny was right behind her, and I knew I was in trouble. Cindy edged close to my side, and without looking at me, she slipped the keys to the truck into my pants pocket. Then Johnny pulled me toward him and whispered harshly, "Have you seen the girls?"

"What girls?"

"You know what girls—the ones who are missing. Do you know where they are?"

"I don't know what you're talking about."

"Don't give me your fucking shit! I saw you and Romano in the hallway where they were."

"Where who were?" I pushed. "I don't know what you're referring to, and I have nothing to do with any girls you're talking about."

I knew he didn't believe me. He yanked me toward him, close enough for his smelly breath to blast my face. He was sweating and convinced that I was involved with the missing girls. He was getting angrier by the second and yelled at me, "I know better than that! Let's see if Romano says the same thing. C'mon," he said as he roughly grabbed my arm, pulling me along with him.

As I turned back to Cindy, I mouthed, "Brian, get Brian." I hoped he was already here and she could find him. I would need him and Mike to come to my rescue.

When we got to the kitchen, Mama was already there. She was a mess—her hair was awry, her dress was wrinkled and pulled up unevenly, and her face was purple with rage. Romano was facing her down, "No one's here. Out! Out! Get out of my kitchen! Now!"

"Not this time, Romano, not this time. Johnny, check out the storage area," she ordered.

Romano was getting apoplectic, "Stop! No one's allowed back there. Get out!"

Mama looked from Romano to me, nodding her head up and down. "I knew we'd find them here."

Romano and I looked at each other but didn't say a word. We could hear Johnny in the storage area, heaving boxes around and making a mess of the room. I was so nervous that I wasn't registering that other than the noise Johnny was creating, there were no sounds from the girls. Several minutes passed, and then Johnny appeared with his face the color of a beet and covered with sweat. He looked at Mama and shook his head. "Nothing."

"I told you so. Now get out of my kitchen!" Both Mama and Johnny reluctantly left. We could hear them hurry back down the hall, and then we heard doors opening and shutting. I was left standing alone with Romano, who was wearing a satisfied smile.

Panicked, I asked, "Where are the girls, Romano?"

"Not to worry," he said. He walked over to the walk-in refrigerator and opened it. I saw four pairs of eyes staring back at me in fear. The girls were shivering but okay.

"How did … ?"

"Cindy warned me. Just in time too."

We held the girls in our arms to warm them and then sat them on the boxes in the storage area. I told them what was going to happen next. Romano was already packing them some food when I slipped out of the kitchen door and ran to the advertising truck. Once in the cab, my hands shook so badly I couldn't fit the key into the ignition and dropped the keys on the floor. I had to dig in the garbage left there by the previous driver until I found them, and scooped them up. Finally, I got the key in the ignition and turned the motor on. I hadn't driven this type of truck before, but I had driven a van, so what could be different? I slowly backed the truck to the kitchen door, and Romano helped me hand the girls inside. Just as the last one was safely in, I put the truck in forward and began my way around the large, mostly empty parking lot to the main street. I was almost there when I saw the valet stand in front of the truck, waving his arms to get me to stop. I was determined to move the girls to safety, so there was no way I would let anyone deter me now. I kept driving. The look on the valet's face as I continued moving toward him was one of complete surprise, which kept him rooted to his spot for a second or two longer than he should have stayed there. He barely had time to jump out of the way—or had I knocked him down?

I drove over the curb and onto the street and kept going. I heard people behind me hollering and saw them running after me. I kept going. I was driving as fast as the truck would go, and we rounded a curve in the road that made the truck stand on the two left wheels. I heard the girls gasp, but then they began to giggle, thinking this was all great fun. One of the younger girls pointed to me and said in Spanish, "Loca." I knew only a few words in Spanish, but this was one I did—crazy! I laughed with them and said, "Yes, you can call me crazy."

Crazy was probably the best word for me at that point. I had stolen a truck and kidnapped four little girls. Where would I hide this oversized truck so we wouldn't be found? I tried to think of a good spot where no one could locate us. I felt a rustle around me and knew it was my grandmother. She whispered, "Parking lot," and off she went. I had no idea what she meant, for we had just come from a parking lot. Then it hit me. Of course.

I knew my way around town pretty well, but I would have to take a chance and see whether I could guess where Gram had meant for me to park. I turned right down the next street, only to end at a dead end. I had to maneuver the truck back and forth several times before I could even turn around. I was beginning to panic. I heard sirens in the background and wondered whether they were for me. I closed my eyes and asked the universe to help keep the girls safe. Where was the spot I was looking for?

As soon as I opened my eyes again, I felt I had to go back down the street I had taken and make the left-hand turn I was supposed to have made in the first place. The road was long and dark because they didn't have regular streetlights in this section of town. I almost passed where I wanted to go, but out of the corner of my eye, I caught a glimpse of the other advertising trucks parked for overnight storage. I backed up a bit and turned into the parking lot. In the darkest part of the lot, I pulled up close to a truck advertising one of the shows on the Strip. I was relieved to have found this spot and whispered, "Thanks, Gram." I parked the truck, and the girls looked at me expectantly. I put my finger to my lips to warn them we had to be quiet.

I felt for my phone in my pants pocket and discovered it wasn't there. Thinking I had lost it when I climbed into the truck, I once again poked through the clutter and grime on the floor but came up empty-handed. No phone. What could I do?

It occurred to me they'd be looking for the truck with the Purple Passion Lounge ad on it, so I gestured to the girls to wait right where they were while I checked the other trucks. I was excited to find the one next to us was unlocked, so the girls and I hopped inside and locked the doors after us. Now, all we had to do was wait.

Human trafficking was becoming a more significant and worse issue in today's society —one to oppose and try to stop completely. I looked at the girls sitting quietly beside me, and my heart filled with love for them. They smiled at me and seemed content despite the predicament we all were in. How could anyone think of selling them or touching them in less-than-loving ways? I knew that because of them, I would get involved in whatever it took to keep them and others like them safe.

I meditated and called out for Brian to find me. I believed that he and Gram had a connection, and maybe it would pay off. I told my grandmother to tell Brian where I was so he could come to save us. I repeatedly whispered, "Brian, we're right here with the other trucks. Come find us and keep us safe." It sounded like an unending mantra, and I could see the girls begin to nod off. It was easy to do because of the quiet darkness.

It wasn't until I heard the gravel crunch underneath the car's tires pulling into the lot that I realized I must have dozed off too. I touched each girl, gestured for silence, and motioned for them to duck down. We soon saw a flashlight shine through the front window and around our truck. We heard voices, but I couldn't identify them.

I had left unlocked the doors of the Purple Passion truck we had used, hoping they'd think we had deserted the area. I heard first one door and then the other open. Both men had flashlights, and they shone them inside. I could hear the men moving things around. One of them called out, "There's nothing here. Let's go back."

"No, we were told to search all the trucks, remember?"

"It's a waste of time, I'm telling you." We heard him say reluctantly, "All right, you start there, and I'll start at the other end. Don't blame me if it's a dead end."

One of the girls whimpered as I heard footsteps getting closer to us. I knew they were terrified, but they had to remain still, or we'd all be in trouble. I reached out to touch her and again put my finger to my lips. I hoped our pursuer's shoes had made enough noise to cover her sound. I held my breath and waited for him to try to open the door on my side.

Then I heard another car enter the parking lot. Soon after, there was another car, and another one followed. The footsteps near me stopped and turned away. I heard a voice yell, "Don't move, or I'll shoot." It was Brian's voice. I let out a sigh of relief.

I listened to a lot of thrashing and heard Brian call out, "Rosie? It's okay; you can come out now."

I opened my door and fell into his arms. I had never been so happy to see anyone in my life. "I'm so glad you made it in time!" I cried out as I collapsed against him.

Pleasantly surprised at my flinging myself at him, he took me into his arms and held me tight. His arms gripped me even more tightly when he saw four sets of eyes watching him. He could see what this escape meant to me and the risk I'd taken to save the children. He bent his head, and he looked into my eyes. He moved closer until his lips met mine. I heard the girls begin to giggle when they saw us kissing. He stepped back just as I took a step back from him. That was something new for us, and we were uncertain what this could mean. We stared at each other, silent until he burst out, "Rosie, you scared me half to death! Don't ever do anything like this again, hear?"

I couldn't help myself. I laughed nervously at the idea that anything like this could happen again. Little did I realize then this was only the beginning of finding myself in situations like this.

I looked over to where Mike was standing, smiling at us. Cindy was by his side, looking pleased to be with him and relieved to see the girls and me safe. She stepped forward. As she got nearer, we hugged each other, hiding our tears of joy and relief.

"I'm so glad you are who you are, my dear friend Cindy."

"I feel the same about you."

Brian's men handcuffed Johnny's men, who had been searching for the girls and me, herded them into their cars, and took them away. I had no idea what would happen to the car they'd left behind. I assumed they were headed for the police station for questioning.

It was time to collect the girls and make our next move. We ended up sending the girls back with Cindy to her house. They would be safe with her until we could have them safely placed with the organization that protects those caught in human trafficking. Perhaps we could reunite them with their families, despite knowing that some families had sold their children for money to keep the rest of the family alive. Many victims came from impoverished families or families struggling with drug addiction, leaving their children to wander and fend for themselves.

I looked at each little girl and hugged her. As they walked away, I gave them the sign language gesture for love. Mike would check in with Cindy later to make sure all was okay.

J.S. Peck

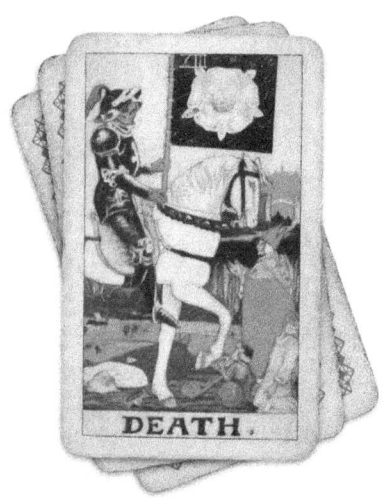

CHAPTER 34

I rode with Brian back to the Purple Passion Lounge to pick up my purse and car. As we drove along, Brian received a phone call, and by the time he hung up, I could tell he was upset.

"What's up? What's wrong?"

My guys have looked every place imaginable and couldn't find the drugs. We know they have to be there somewhere. The snitch told us the drugs were delivered today, but where are they? Were they offloaded already? That doesn't seem possible, especially with all that's been happening."

I had no answer. We rode in silence until we arrived, and there were police cars everywhere. "What happened to all the men there for the little girls? Have they all been arrested?"

"They all have been taken to the police station. Because of who they are, they'll hire high-priced lawyers to convince the judge their clients had no idea children were involved in the 'appreciation buffet" given for the lounge's best clients. It's all legal. You know how that works, don't you?"

"Unfortunately, I do," I responded, downhearted.

As we drove up to the lounge, Mama was outside, handcuffed, and held by one of the police officers. The man standing beside her turned out to be the Chief of Police, a man I hated with a passion. As I stepped from the car, both of them approached me. A look of intense hatred crossed Mama's face as she spat at me. "If you think you can ruin me, let me tell you something. That's not going to happen." She turned to the Chief of Police before continuing, "Don't even think of pinning that story about the little girls on me. Rosalie, you're the one who set that up, aren't you? You thought you and your chef friend could make some money on the side, right?"

I was bewildered by her accusations. "What are you talking about?"

"You know what I'm talking about. Arrest her, Franklin!"

"Now, Bertha, you know we must do things the right way …."

"Hold on. What's going on here?" Brian asked as he pulled me away from the two of them.

Mike came up beside me and said, "Let's get her inside."

The three of us left them behind and walked inside. "Where's Romano? Is he okay?" I asked.

Mike grinned, "I think he's going to have a big, beautiful black eye. After you left, Johnny came back into the kitchen and started arguing with him. He grabbed Romano and punched him in the eye. In turn, Romano grabbed a frying pan and knocked Johnny out. We found him out cold on the floor."

I ran into the kitchen to find Romano sitting on one of the steel stools, holding a steak against his left eye. "I'm so sorry, Romano, for all the trouble I caused you. Are you okay?"

Romano looked up at me with a smile on his face. "Ah, my little Rosebud! You gave me a scare the way you tore out of here. I wasn't sure you would make it with those little girls."

"It's because of you that they are safe. You're my hero, for sure," I said with tears. I put my arms around his shoulders and kissed him on each cheek. None of that air-kissing this time.

Romano looked around the kitchen, and when he saw the disarray, he implored, "Why do they have to mess it up? Why can't people stay out of my kitchen? "

His pleadings gave me an idea. "Romano, why did Johnny come back into the kitchen?"

"He said that he was looking for what belonged to him. I told him the girls didn't belong to anyone. Then, of course, we fought over it." Romano began to smile. "I got him good, though, didn't I?"

"You sure did," I answered, smiling at his pleasure.

Brian and Mike were amused as they stood there watching us. I turned to them and said, "I know where your drugs are."

Both of them looked at me in disbelief.

"Yup," I said, "and Romano will help you find them."

"I will?" asked Romano.

"Yup. Would you please go get your delivery ticket from this morning?"

Romano handed it to me, and we headed into the storage area with Brian and Mike behind us. We began to check off what was on the list and compared it with what wasn't listed. There it was! One box was supposed to be cans of tomato sauce, but once we opened a can, we found it filled with what looked like heroin.

"How did you know, Rosie?" asked Brian.

"Several years back, they caught a woman 'enthralled' by a Mafia bigwig in Australia. Barbaro was his name, I think. The woman was the gofer for his crime syndicate, responsible for the shipment of 4.4 tons of Ecstasy worth more than $122 million hidden in 3,000 cans of tomatoes."

"How did you remember that?"

I laughed. "I don't care for tomatoes. I've never forgotten this story because, at the time, I thought it was hysterical to think tomatoes could provide anyone ecstasy. That was before I'd eaten some of Romano's food, of course," I smiled.

Romano smiled at me and held his fingers together in a perfecto sign. We all were on a high. I was over the moon, excited that it was over. We'd succeeded in finding the drugs and could take down those responsible for it. "Well, guys, we have our man, so to speak. It's a good feeling to take down Mama and all she was up to."

All three men nodded in agreement. However, the hand-slapping and congratulations died once I added, "But all of this has nothing to do with clearing up the murders of Melissa, Sally, or Sam. It's not over yet, is it?"

We all looked at one another. No one said a word. I walked out of the kitchen to grab my purse and head home. I had a lot to mull over. Yes, we successfully found the heroin, which had been delivered that morning, and we now had a solid trail leading to where the drugs were coming from. We knew in time that all the accusations of who was supplying the drugs and distributing them would eventually come to light because experience has shown that each involved wants to save their own skin. Anyway, that's how it worked most times.

It seemed that this time it was Mama who would be taking the fall, not only for the drugs but also for trafficking the little girls. We each knew that she alone was not responsible for all that had happened, but things don't always turn out the way they should. I knew that because of what had happened to Jeff. I was surprised to feel a little sorry for Mama—or maybe it was simply because she was in the same situation Jeff had been in, with no one stepping forward to challenge her pegged as the only one involved.

As I walked back down the hall from the employees' lounge, I passed the doorway to the kitchen area. I saw Brian and Mike turn my way, each with concern for me on their face. They were so handsome. I felt my heart beat faster. I was happy to know we would continue working together, for things were left to do, and I wondered what would happen after we had cleared up the murders. Would we still be in each other's lives?

I thought of Melissa, Sally, and Sam. I had no intention of forgetting them and was determined to discover who had taken their lives. I was realistic enough to understand it would take a lot more effort and time to resolve their murders. But I'd do whatever it took.

I whispered to their spirits, "No worries, my friends, remember, 'it ain't over til it's over.'"

J.S. Peck

CHECK OUT THE NEXT BOOK IN
THE DEATH CARD SERIES

DEATH
AT THE LAKE

Book 2

The Death Card Series

By

J.S. Peck

BEJEWELED PUBLISHING
LAS VEGAS, NEVADA

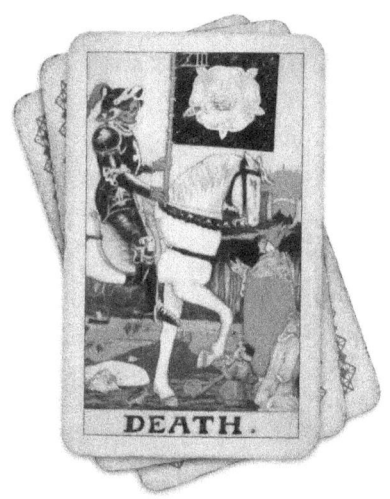

CHAPTER 1

As soon as I pushed through the door, I raced into the living room and threw myself on the couch. I grabbed a pillow and screamed into it. I cried, laughed hysterically, and cried hard enough to cause hiccups. I was a total hot mess—exhilarated and exhausted. I was emotionally done.

I had to credit Sweet Pea, my darling dog, who sat at my feet. She never moved as she watched my antics. I thought she knew I was in trouble, big trouble. I'd worked undercover at the Purple Passion Lounge to help solve the murders of a client and another dancer who performed there. Instead of nailing the murderers, I'd participated in a drug bust and kidnapped four little girls the lounge managers had brought in to sell in their human trafficking scheme.

Even today, all I have to do is close my eyes to see the little girls' four sets of eyes staring back at me as they had when I unlocked one of the office doors and found them hiding inside. What was going to happen to them? What about me for having kidnapped them? The Chief of Police wasn't about to let me off the hook for that. What about those people who'd love to get their hands on me for interfering with their plan? What was happening with the three different murders yet to be solved?

Everything would have to wait; I couldn't worry about it now. I needed to get to bed and begin to recuperate. It was my turn to host my three best friends here in Las Vegas, and they'd be here in less than 24 hours. Nothing was going to keep me from that. Most importantly, for our safety, I couldn't tell them how much I was involved in all that was happening here with the murders. That would be hard to do because we usually had no secrets between us.

The following day, I awoke feeling slightly better. As I lay in bed, I mentally listed what I'd need to do before my friends arrived. But before I could get out of bed to start, the doorbell rang, and Sweet Pea raced down the stairs to greet whoever was at the door. As I followed her, she barked excitedly and wagged her tail. When I opened the door, there was Brian, my investigative partner, with a worried look. He looked so handsome standing there. Despite our appearing to be opposites, I was attracted to him, but neither wanted to be tied down at this point in our lives. We each enjoyed our freedom to do what we wanted. That was our "push me, pull you" sort of relationship.

"Hi, there, Cowboy! What's up?"

Coming straight to the point, he asked, "Your friends are coming in today, right?"

"Not until tonight."

"Okay, that still works." He looked intently at me, unsure, before continuing, "I've made arrangements for you and your friends, even Sweet Pea, to share a double room suite for the next three days at Loews out at Lake Las Vegas."

"Whoa!" I shook my head in protest.

He immediately held up his hand and said, "It's on me! I've already paid for it; it'll cost you nothing—meals and libations included. Your presence there will keep you safe and away from here until things settle down."

"Thanks, but no thanks. We're staying right here at my house. Besides, why would you do that?"

"We still have things to clean up, and I don't want you involved. The people we think are entangled in all the murders know where you live, remember?"

"Do you mean you have a lead on who killed Melissa and Sally?" I asked, my curiosity mounting. I didn't want to be left out of discovering and prosecuting the people responsible for their deaths. From the first, I vowed to do that and still wanted to be a part of it.

"We're working on it, but there's no room for you to be involved," he repeated emphatically before throwing in the last incentive, "Besides, the last thing you want to do is hurt your girlfriends, right?"

He had me there. I hated to give in, but I could see his point. "If I agree, I don't want you to pay for anything. I'll take care of it myself."

"Too bad; it's already done. You can pay for the other things you girls do, okay?"

"I've already purchased tickets to see a show at The Smith Center on one of the nights …."

"No problem," he immediately cut in. "I'll have a limo pick you up. Just let me know the day and time."

"Just how are you managing to do all this, if you don't mind my asking?"

"Well, I *do* mind," he said firmly, dismissing any chance of a response. "Promise me you'll leave first thing in the morning, Rosie. Enjoy it out there."

As I hesitated, he added, "You deserve a break from all this! Get a massage or a—what do you girls call it?—a mani-pedi or something? Just *stay there* and have *fun.*"

I stood in front of him and weighed the pros and cons. He interrupted my train of thought by adding, "I'll have security there for you too. But if anything comes up or you need me, call me right away. Just go and enjoy," he insisted.

Hmmm. Although I wasn't feeling entirely comfortable about his proposition, maybe this wouldn't be such a bad idea after all. I was more than a little worried I might have more unwelcome visitors here at the house while my friends were staying with me. I certainly didn't want them to be involved or get hurt.

"Well? Promise me?" He paused. "Just tell them you won a prize or something," he coached.

"Okay, deal," I said reluctantly as we shook hands. Then Brian pulled me forward and looked deep into my eyes. He ended up kissing me on the forehead. "What's up with that?" I wondered.

He bent down to pat Sweet Pea before he turned to leave. "I've paid the guard at the gate to keep careful watch over your house tonight and for the next few days. Call me right away if anything more happens. I mean it."

I stood there not knowing what to say, so I said nothing as he walked out the door. I wasn't used to all this concern or relying on someone else. Sometimes it made me feel like I was floating along, doing what anyone wanted, and I didn't have a choice. Maybe this time, I didn't.

I looked at the clock and realized I would have to redo my shopping list to buy different treats to take to Lake Las Vegas. Sunscreen, beach towels, and more. I would also have to pack for Sweet Pea, who'd be overjoyed and excited about joining us. She loves staying at hotels and acting as the official greeter of the guests, whether anyone wants her to be or not. Luckily, she's cute enough to get away with it.

The day sped by, and before I knew it, it was time to pick up my "sister-friends" at the airport. They managed their flight times to land just about 20 minutes apart, making it easy for everyone to gather before heading together to my house.

My sister-friends (more like sisters than friends) and I always had fun together, doing whatever inspired us at the time. We never knew what would happen, making it even more crazy fun. I was lucky enough to attend Cornell College, where I met and befriended these three fabulous women—two from Boston, Massachusetts, and one from Boise, Idaho. When I was younger, they were the ones who'd alleviated the pain of my having been belittled and bullied for my and my grandmother's psychic abilities.

I loved my girlfriends, for they filled my life in ways so fantastic it's hard to describe. I couldn't wait to see them. The first to arrive was Nancy from Boise. At first, she was hard to find in the crowd because she was petite, only five feet tall. It is her wild blond, curly hair sticking out between the taller people that made me able to pull her from the line and hug her. My 5'10" dwarfed her, but her smile was huge and electrifying, making me so grateful she was my friend. She is a tomboy who loves all sports and animals. She even owns four non-allergenic dogs of her own. At college, she took courses to become a veterinarian, but her allergies to animals kept her from working with them daily. Instead, she works from home for the offices of an organization that fundraises to protect endangered animals around the globe. She loves her job and has traveled worldwide to see some of these animals, always taking her allergy medicine.

We chatted away while we waited for Karen and Susannah to arrive. Nancy showed me pictures of her newest puppy and videos of all four dogs playing together. They were hysterical.

Then, we heard a tremendous shout—"Helloooo!"—so we knew Karen was here. She's the unrestrained "kid" who finds fun in almost everything she does. Karen teaches first grade—no surprise—and has won several awards for her way with children and for helping international students settle into America and the English language. She was dancing her way toward us, waving her arms in the air above her head. "I'm so glad to be here, ladies. We're going to have so much fun together."

We exchanged hugs and kisses, and Susannah showed up, looking as trim and professional as possible. She is the "perfectionist" who always wants everything to be in order. Susannah had a rough childhood and has a control issue, but she knows that about herself and can laugh at her ways. She's a corporate lawyer working in the financial district in Boston, dressing and looking the part in all the best ways. Other people often find Susannah intimidating, but we three don't. Susannah can be a hoot, for she has a very dry sense of humor. We love to be in her company.

After collecting our things, we drove to my house. "So, what's happening, Rosie? Anything exciting?" asked Nancy as we entered the house.

I remained silent as Sweet Pea came running, barking her pleasure at seeing the girls. She was convinced, I think, they'd come just for her. Sweet Pea was their gift to me after

Jeff died; luckily, she is loved by all and treated like one of the girls. Because she is non-allergenic, Nancy immediately swooped her up in her arms and received many kisses. The other girls pampered her as well. Sweet Pea looked up at me with a massive smile on her face. When I first had her, it took me time to realize that, yes, indeed, dogs really can smile.

"Hold on, girls. Don't unpack your bags yet."

"Woo-hoo!" Karen cried out. "A surprise. When we talked the other night, I knew you were up to something special. I could hear it in your voice."

"Well, I *do* have a surprise for all of us. We head out tomorrow. We were given a double suite for three days at Loews at Lake Las Vegas. Even Sweet Pea was invited," I added.

"Woo-hoo!" hollered Nancy. "I love that place. Isn't that the same one we drove out to see and have cocktails the last time we were here?

"It sure is," answered Karen. "I wouldn't forget a place like that."

"Ladies, let's go upstairs," I said. "In the first guest room are your presents for this trip."

"Wow—more surprises?" asked Karen.

"Are you sure you want to spend your money like this?" inquired Susannah in an aside whisper. She's my lawyer and handles most of my financial affairs dealing with my trust fund. She asked me despite knowing I had more than enough money to do this and anything else I wanted, thanks to my parents and Grandmother's keen investment sense.

"This is a thank-you for doing a favor for a special client," I informed them. "Room and board are on the house; all else is on us. Not bad, huh?" I hated not telling the truth, much less calling Brian a client.

"I'll say. I sure would love to meet your client," enthused Karen.

"You never know ..." I responded in a low voice.

Excited as little girls, we hurried up the stairs and piled into the first guest room. Four bundles, alike except for the color of the beach towels, were on the bed. "Just pick one, and I'll take what's left," I encouraged them.

Each girl grabbed a pack, and we laughed because we were all comparing what we had to the others. This behavior hasn't changed since our early days of college and many fun get-togethers. We all tried on the hats, and Nancy and Karen switched theirs.

In addition to a beach towel, each bundle held a matching t-shirt with "Girlfriends are the BEST" written on it, a summer reading romance paperback, suntan lotion (for Susannah's dark skin, too), after-sun cream, and fruit lip gloss. Each person's things fit into one of the tan straw bags, which had colored handles that matched the color of the beach towels. That way, we'd be able to tell which one was whose. Since we'd share the books, we were satisfied with what we had.

"Let's head downstairs for a nightcap before we go to bed," I suggested. "How does Amaretto on the rocks sound?"

Karen said, "Now we're talking." She's not a real drinker but loves to indulge when she's with the rest of us.

Nancy and Susannah chimed in together, "Count me in."

We settled in for some small talk before heading to bed. The next day at Lake Las Vegas would be the start of our sister-friends weekend, and we couldn't wait for it to begin.

J.S. PECK

Joan was reared in a family of readers in small-town Elmira, New York. When she was growing up, each Sunday afternoon was a special time when each family member relaxed with a good book. "It was when I began reading the Nancy Drew series that mysteries intrigued me.

"To me, the fun of reading mystery books is to become so involved with the story it becomes impossible to put the book down. A good mystery has often caused me to stay up all night to finish it to see whether I can figure out whodunit. For anyone hooked on reading mystery books, there's nothing better than that."

In addition, Joan was raised to be open-minded and understood that we are all connected energetically and can communicate with others who have passed on. She brings that idea into her Death Card series by having the spirit of Rosie's grandmother pop into her life with advice or loving messages. Rosie is portrayed as a psychic, meaning she has visions of what is yet to come.

Joan also writes books under the name Joan S. Peck, and that website is www.JoanSPeck.com.

I hope you enjoy reading this book and the entire Death Card series. If you did, please help other readers discover it by leaving a review on Amazon.com. I thank you for your kindness.

—Joan

ACKNOWLEDGMENTS

Many thanks to all those in my family and others who have supported me on my journey to writing mysteries. It's heartwarming to have your encouragement.

From the bottom of my heart, I thank all of you who picked up this book to read. I hope you find enjoyment in every chapter and, even more so, find this book difficult to put down. That's what a good mystery is all about.

To all of you first readers, I can't thank you enough for taking time to plow through the book's first version. I appreciate Doreen Ping, Donna Stidman, Karen Coltin, Ann Frazier, Sharon Caldwell, Anne Heim, Marquetta Goodwin, and Rick Purvine.

What makes a good book great? Editing. So with great appreciation for their talent, I thank Shelly Peck, Judi Moreo, and my editor extraordinaire, Meredith Reed. Kudos and gratitude to you all.

I was blessed the day I contacted Kelly Martin to be my book cover designer. Thank you, Kelly, for your creativity and artistic talents. I love your work.

Thank you, Jake Naylor, for designing my website, being my layout person, and so much more. You're a marvel, and you're the best.

BOOKS BY J.S. PECK

THE DEATH CARD SERIES
- Book 1: *Death on the Strip*
- Book 2: *Death at the Lake*
- Book 3: *Death Returns*
- Book 4: *Death in the Shadows*
- Book 5: *Death on the Run*
- Book 6: *Death Comes Calling*

A HOLIDAY ROMANCE SERIES
- Book 1: *Santa Baby*
- Book 2: *Presents from Heaven*

ROMANTIC MYSTERIES
- *Angels Out of the Dark*
- *The Waiting Room*
- *The Boston Fiasco*

BOOKS BY JOAN S. PECK

- *The Seven Major Chakras – Keeping it Simple*
- *A Simple Approach to Living a Successful Life*
- *What You Need to Know to Live a Spiritual Life*
- *Prime Threat – Shattering the Power of Addiction*